AMERICAN GOLEM

The New World Adventures of an Old World Mud Monster

BY
MARC
LUMER

APPLES & HONEY PRESS

To my son Benny
To my parents, Gunter & Linda Lumer ע"ה, -M.L.

Apples & Honey Press
An imprint of Behrman House
Millburn, New Jersey 07041

www.applesandhoneypress.com

ISBN 978-1-68115-535-7

Library of Congress Cataloging-in-Publication Data

Names: Lumer, Marc, author, illustrator.
Title: American golem : the new world adventures of
an old world mud monster
 / by Marc Lumer.
Description: Millburn, New Jersey : Apples & Honey
Press, [2018]
Identifiers: LCCN 2017019298 | ISBN 9781681155357
Classification: LCC PZ7.1.L847 Ame 2018 | DDC
[E]--dc23 LC record available at https://lccn.loc.
gov/2017019298

The publisher wishes to acknowledge the following
sources of photographs:
The New York Public Library Digital Collection/
New York World's Fair 17, 24; The New York
Public Library Digital Collection/Berenice
Abbott 36; U.S. National Library of Medicine 39.

GREEN GOLD
Animation Corporation

Illustrated in collaboration with the artists at
Design by Marc Lumer
Edited by Dena Neusner

Printed in the United States of America

9 8 7 6 5 4 3 2

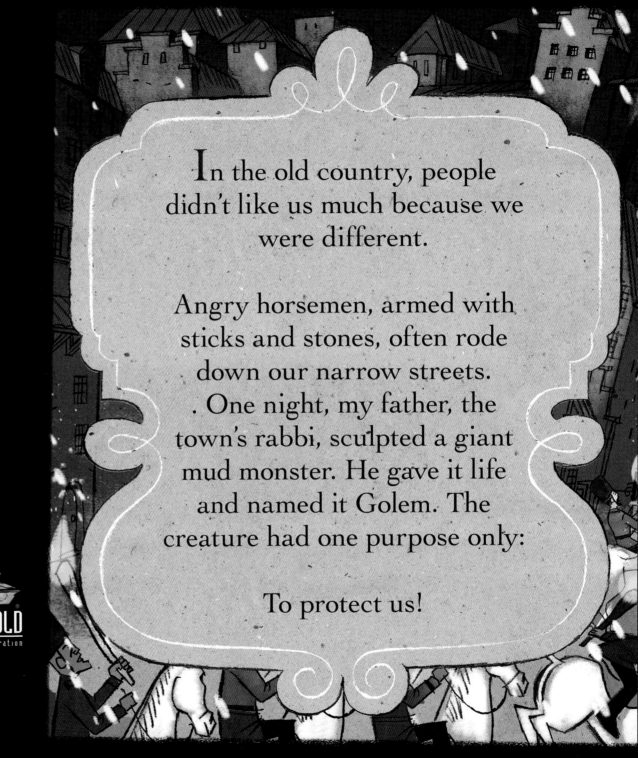

In the old country, people didn't like us much because we were different.

Angry horsemen, armed with sticks and stones, often rode down our narrow streets. One night, my father, the town's rabbi, sculpted a giant mud monster. He gave it life and named it Golem. The creature had one purpose only:

To protect us!

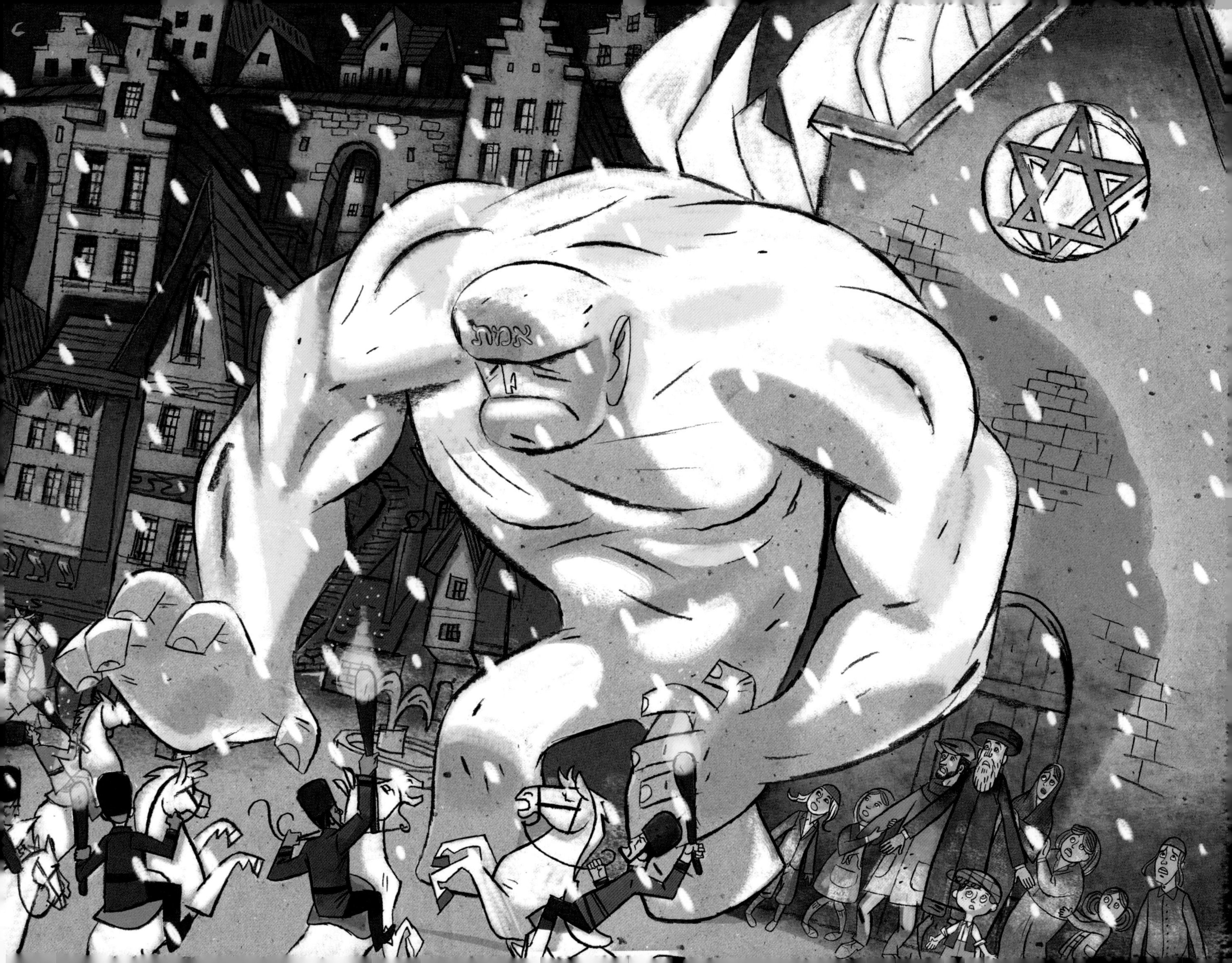
אמת

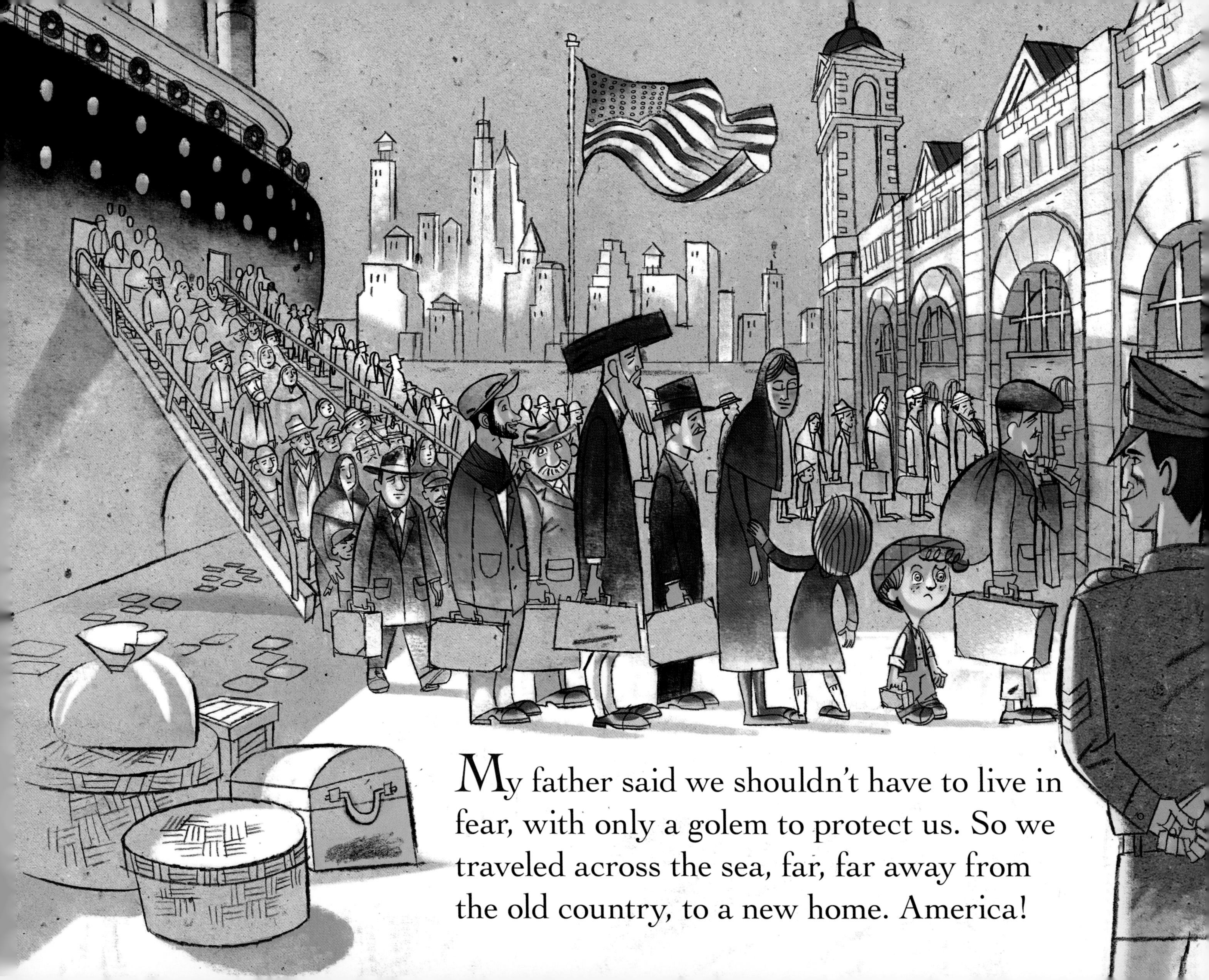

My father said we shouldn't have to live in fear, with only a golem to protect us. So we traveled across the sea, far, far away from the old country, to a new home. America!

In America everything was big,

and crowded,

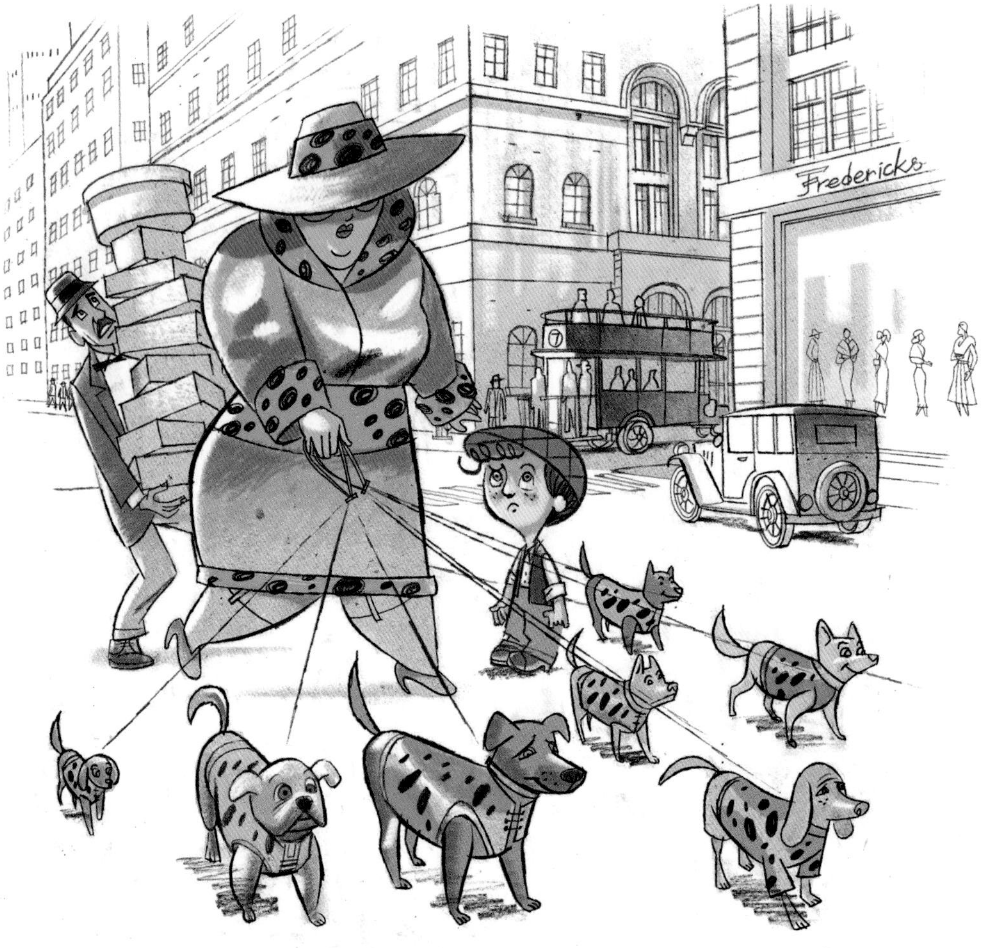
Fredericks

and strange,

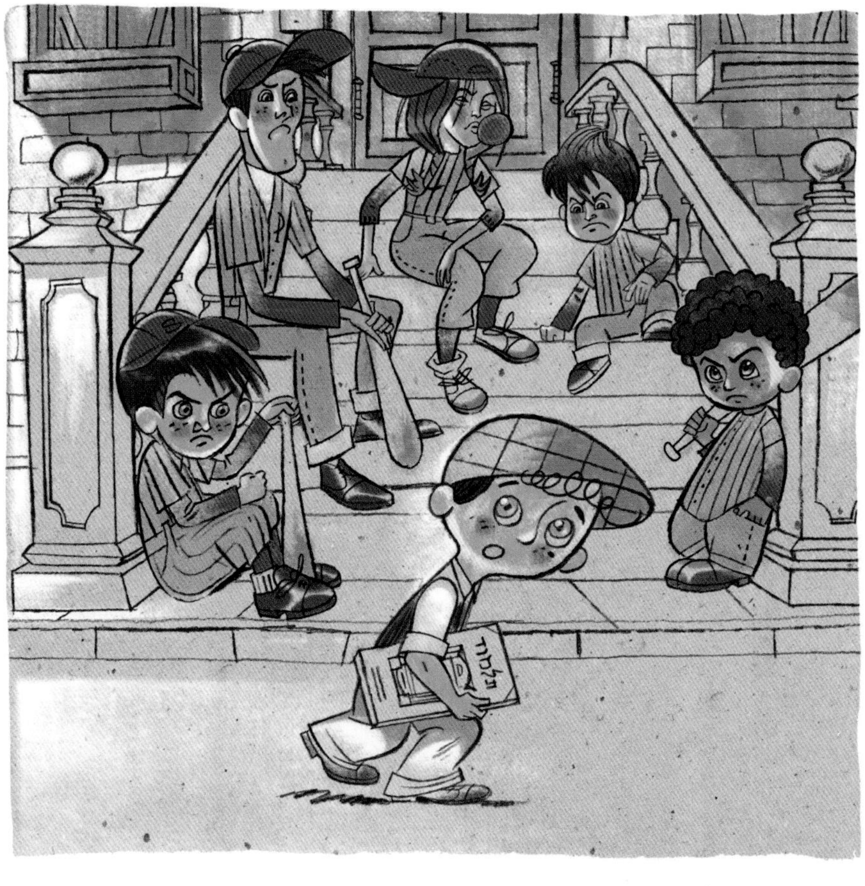

and scary!

Scariest of all were the kids next door. As soon as they saw me...

...they ran after me, yelling, "Hey you, hey kid! Wait!"

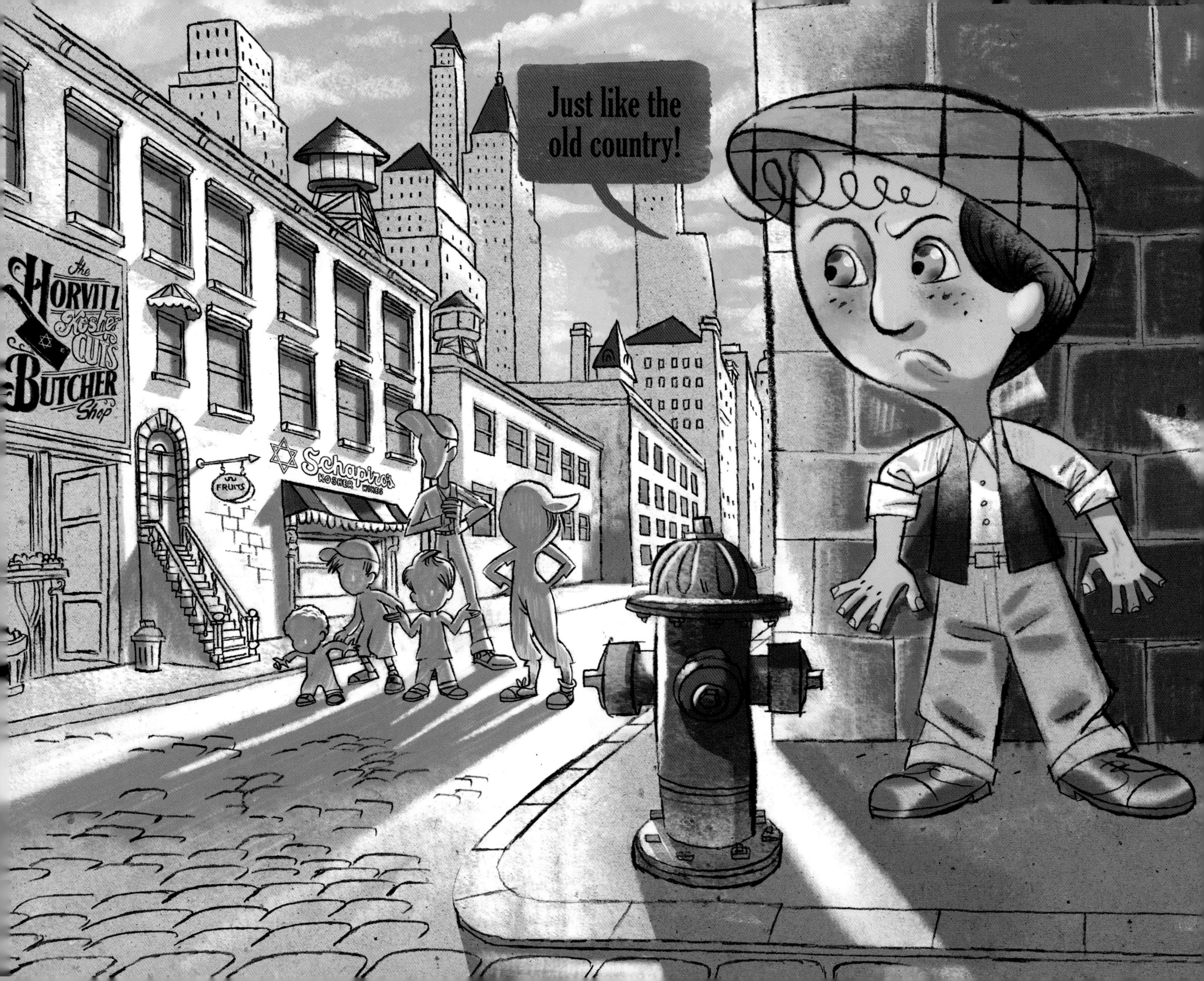
Just like the old country!
the HORVITZ Kosher CUTS BUTCHER Shop
FRUITS
Schapiro's KOSHER WINES

Luckily for me, we had brought some useful books with us.

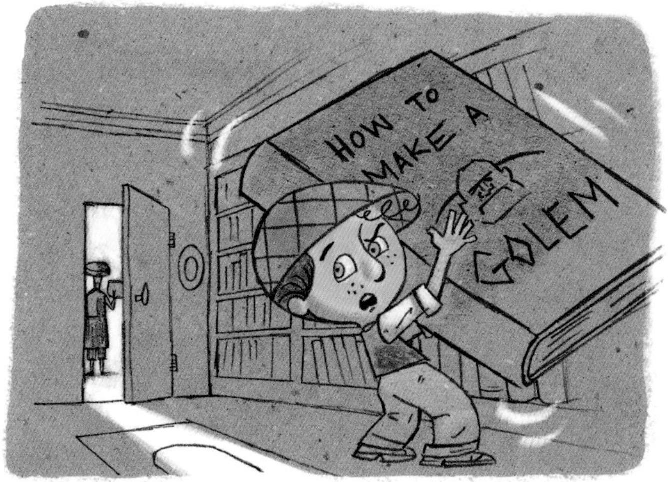

HOW TO MAKE A GOLEM

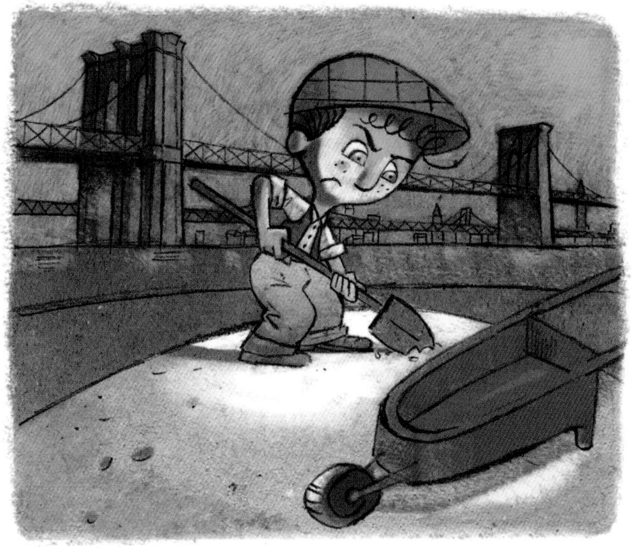

A little bit of mud,

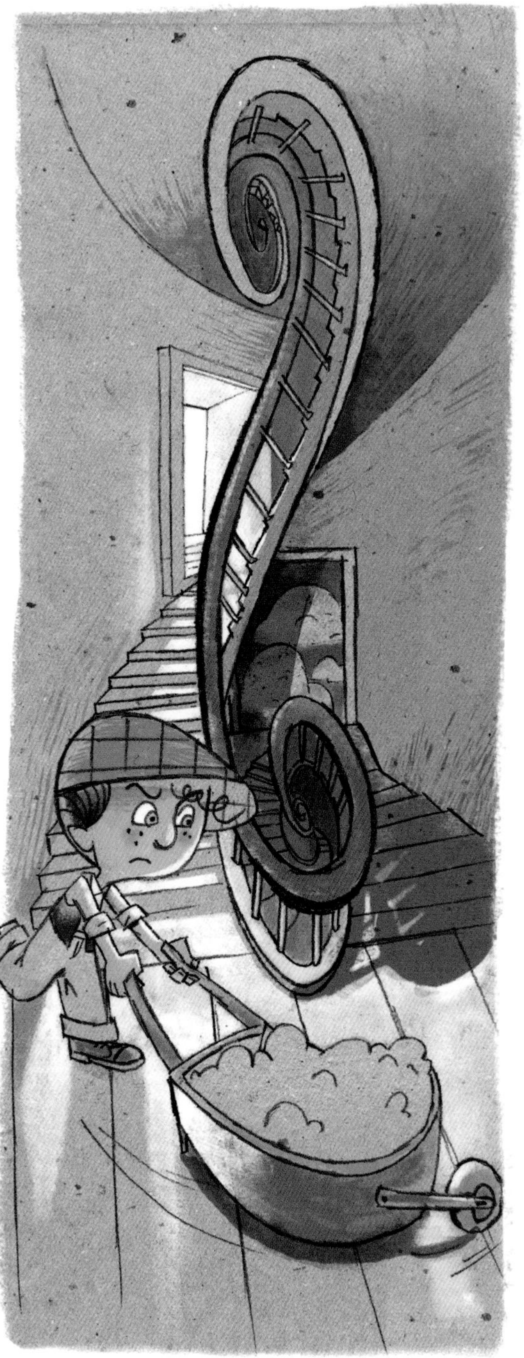

a quiet place to work,

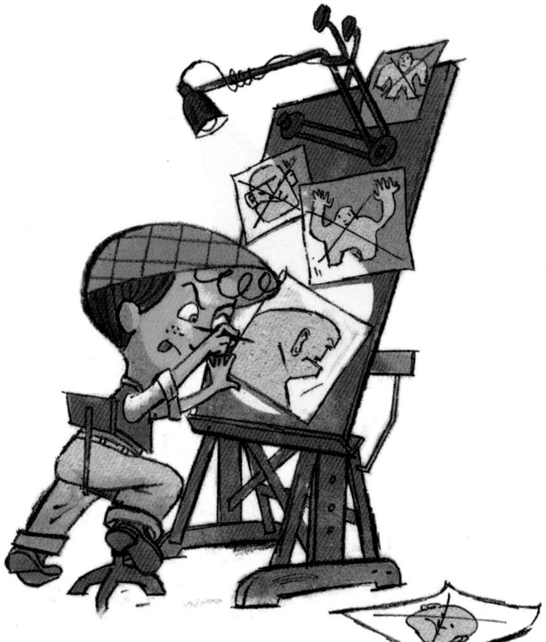

a good design,

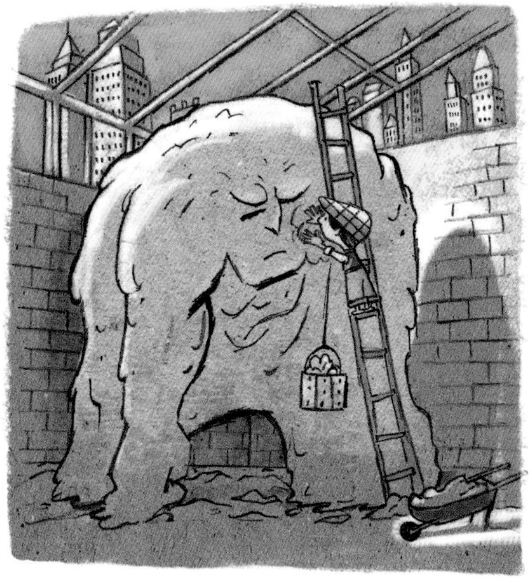

a bit of elbow grease,

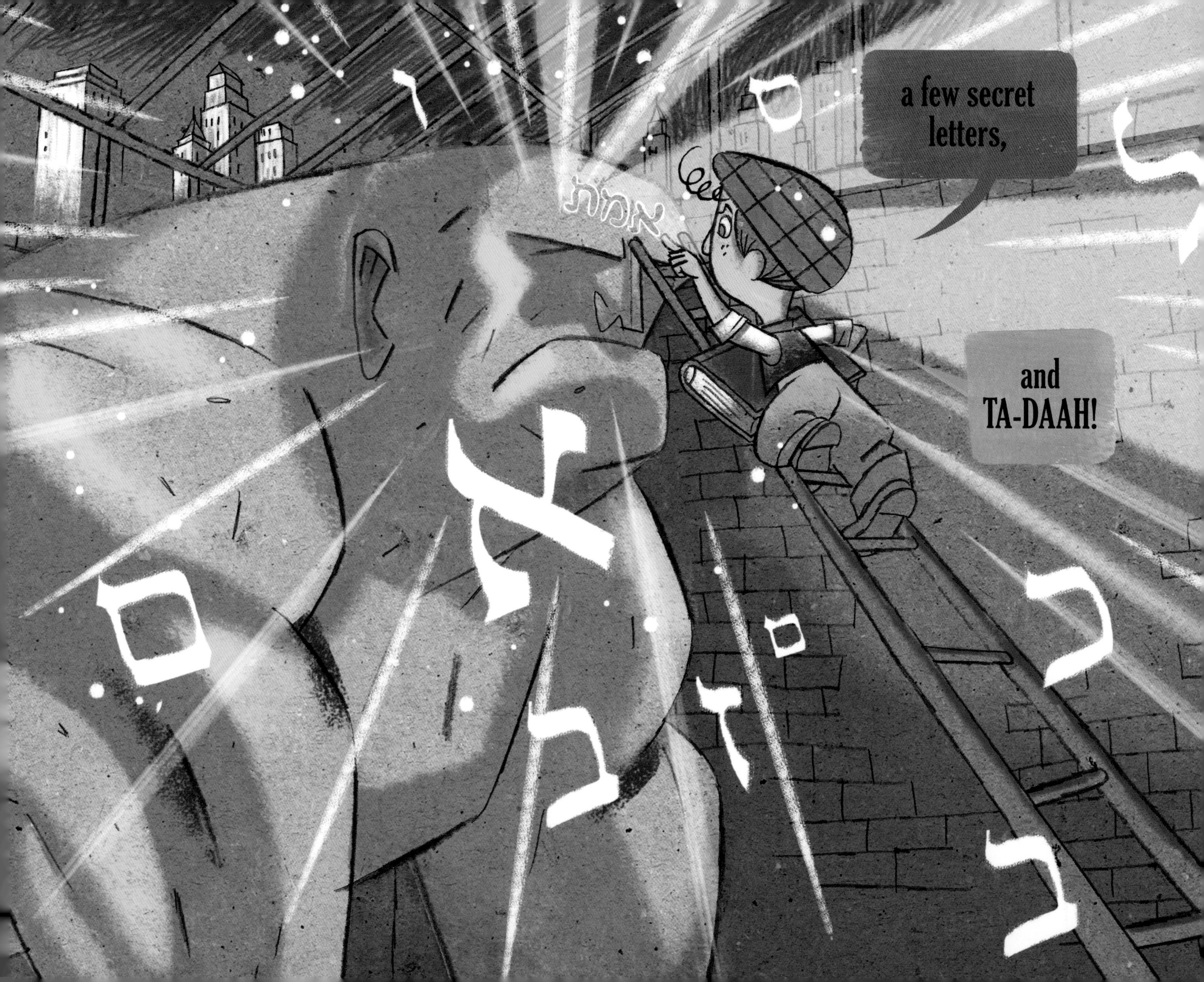
אמת
a few secret letters,
and TA-DAAH!

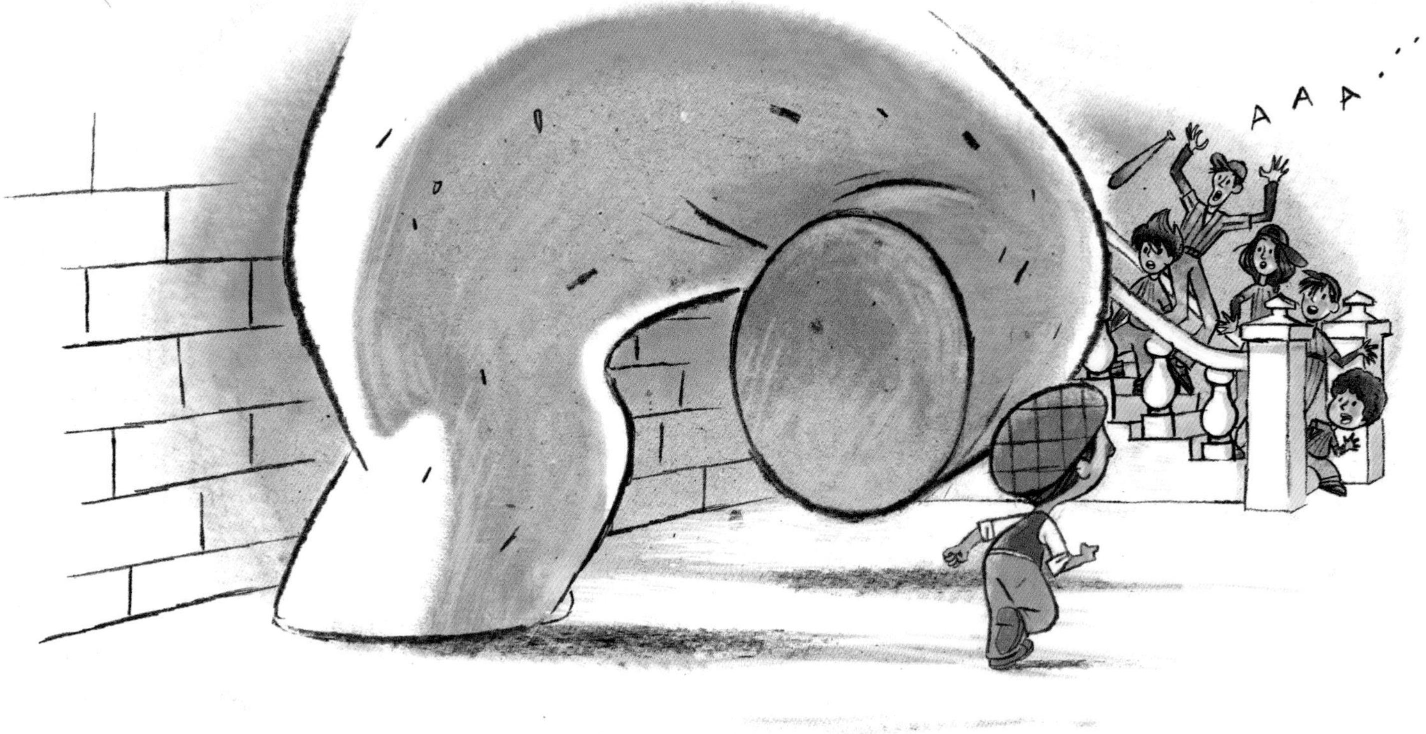
AAA...

Now I had my own golem to protect me!

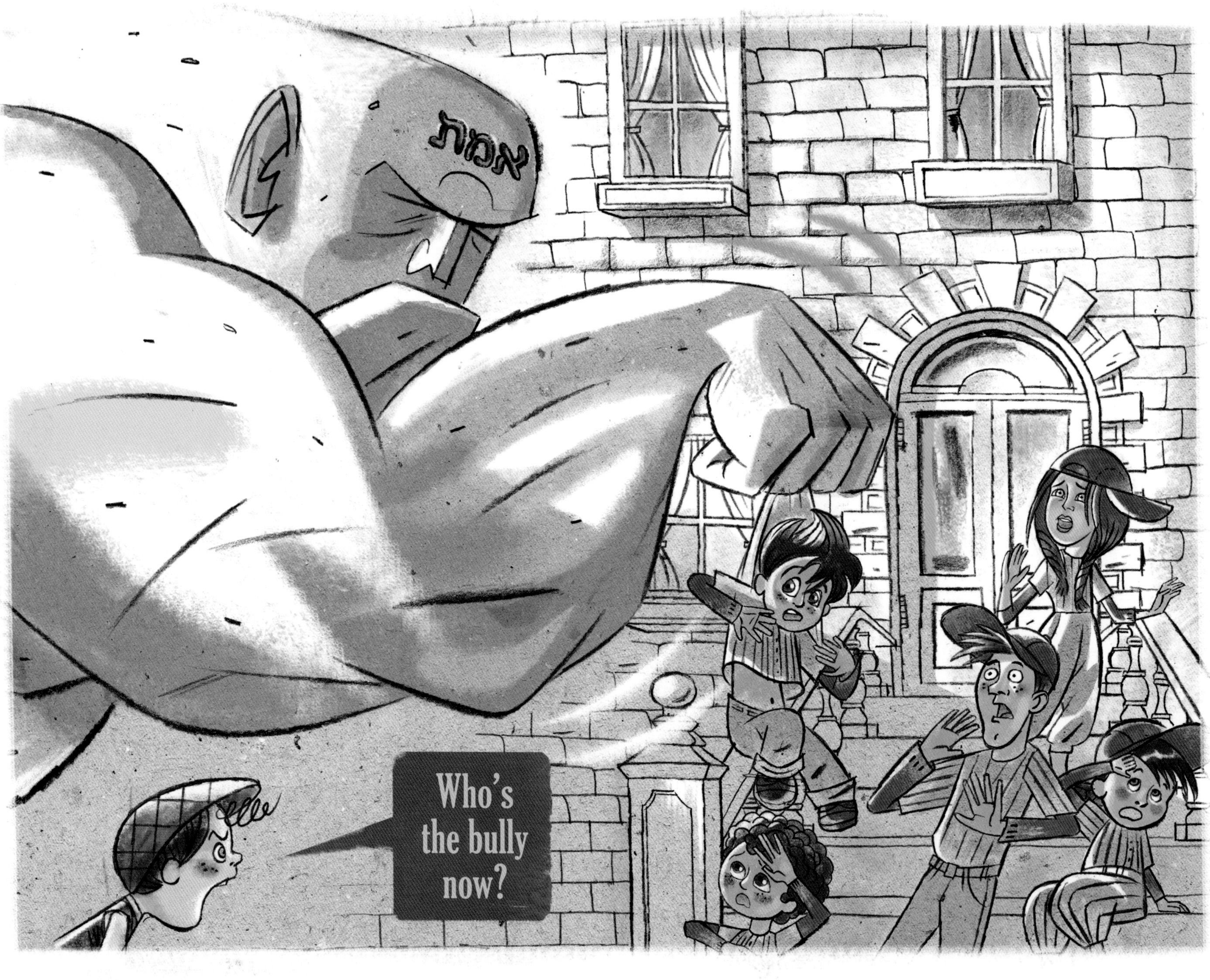
אמת
Who's the bully now?

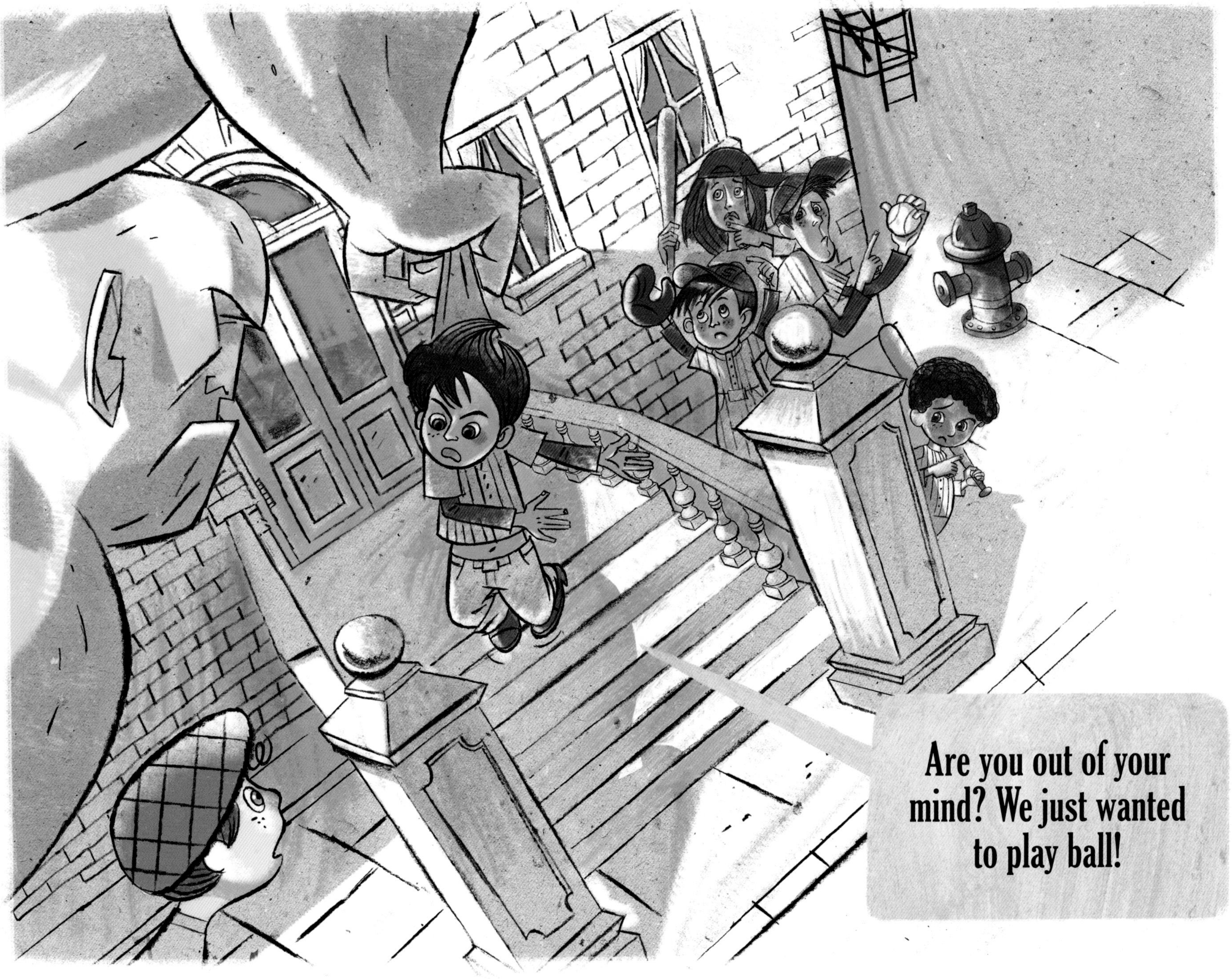
Are you out of your mind? We just wanted to play ball!

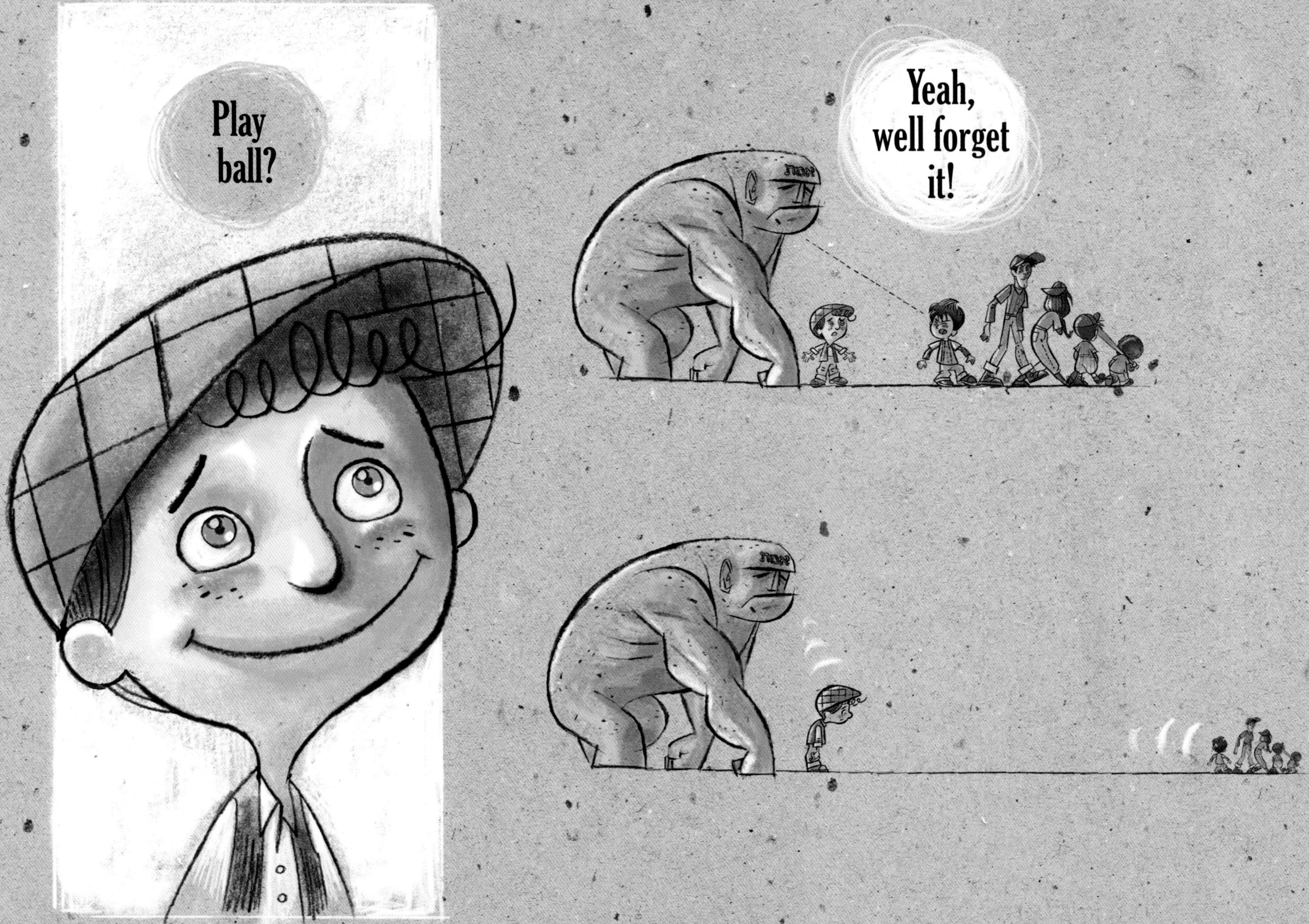
Play ball?
Yeah, well forget it!

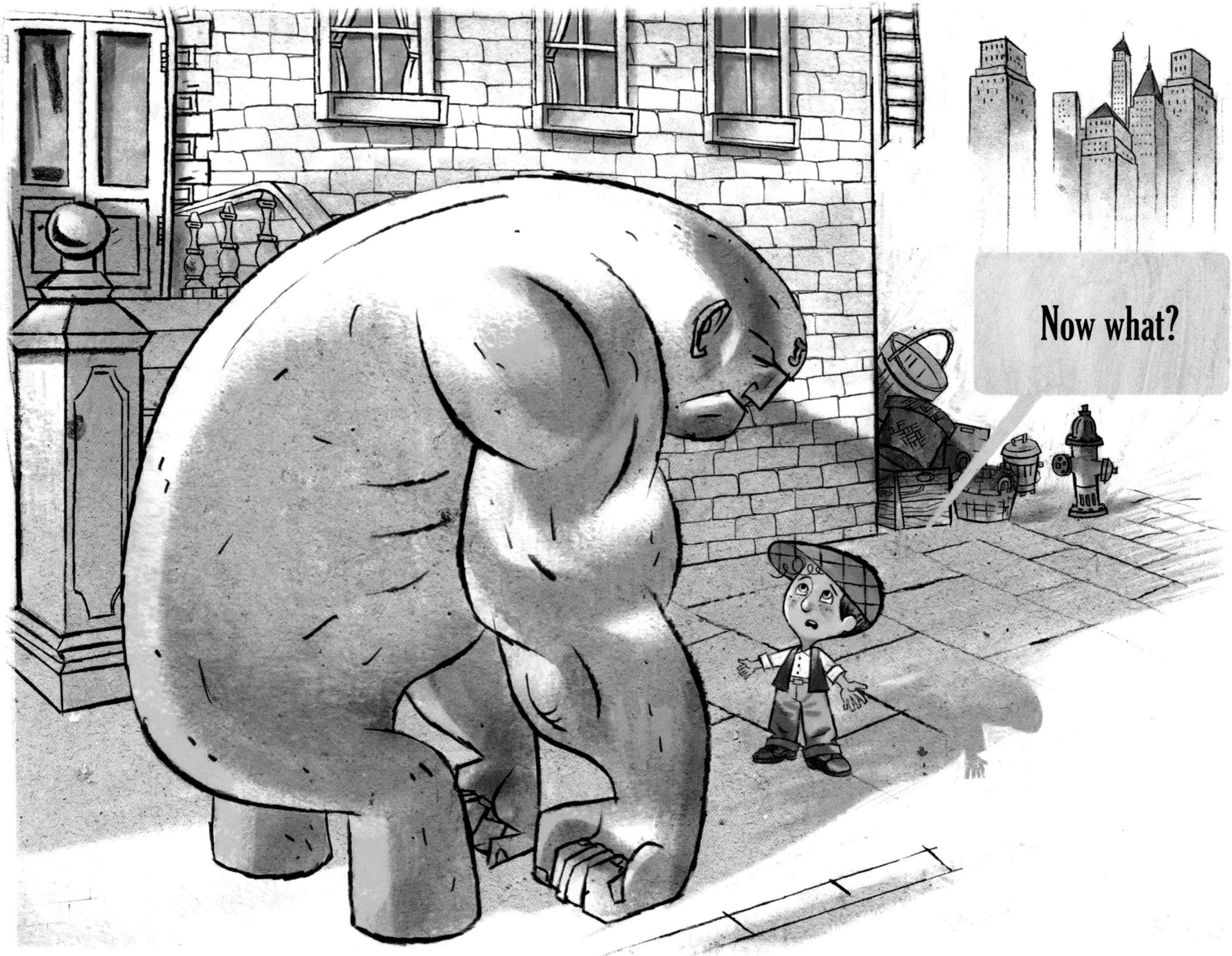
Now what?

What would my golem do with no one to protect? I had to find him a purpose!

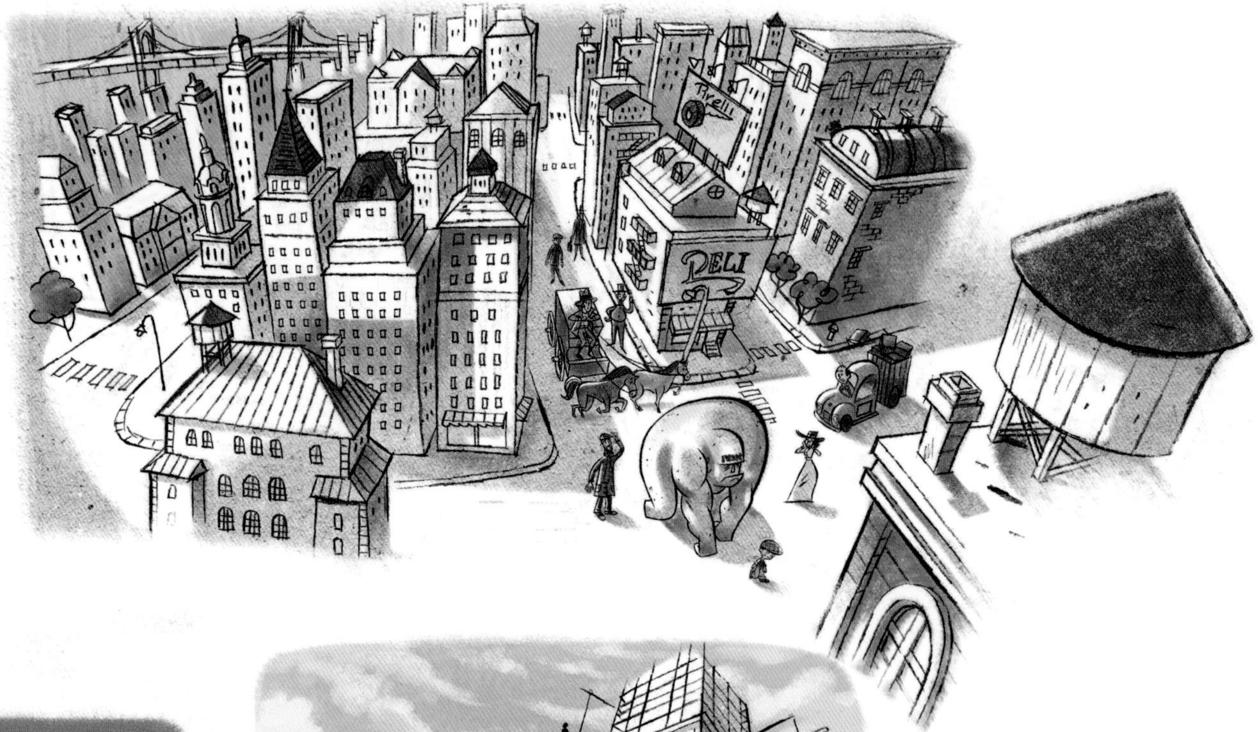
DELI

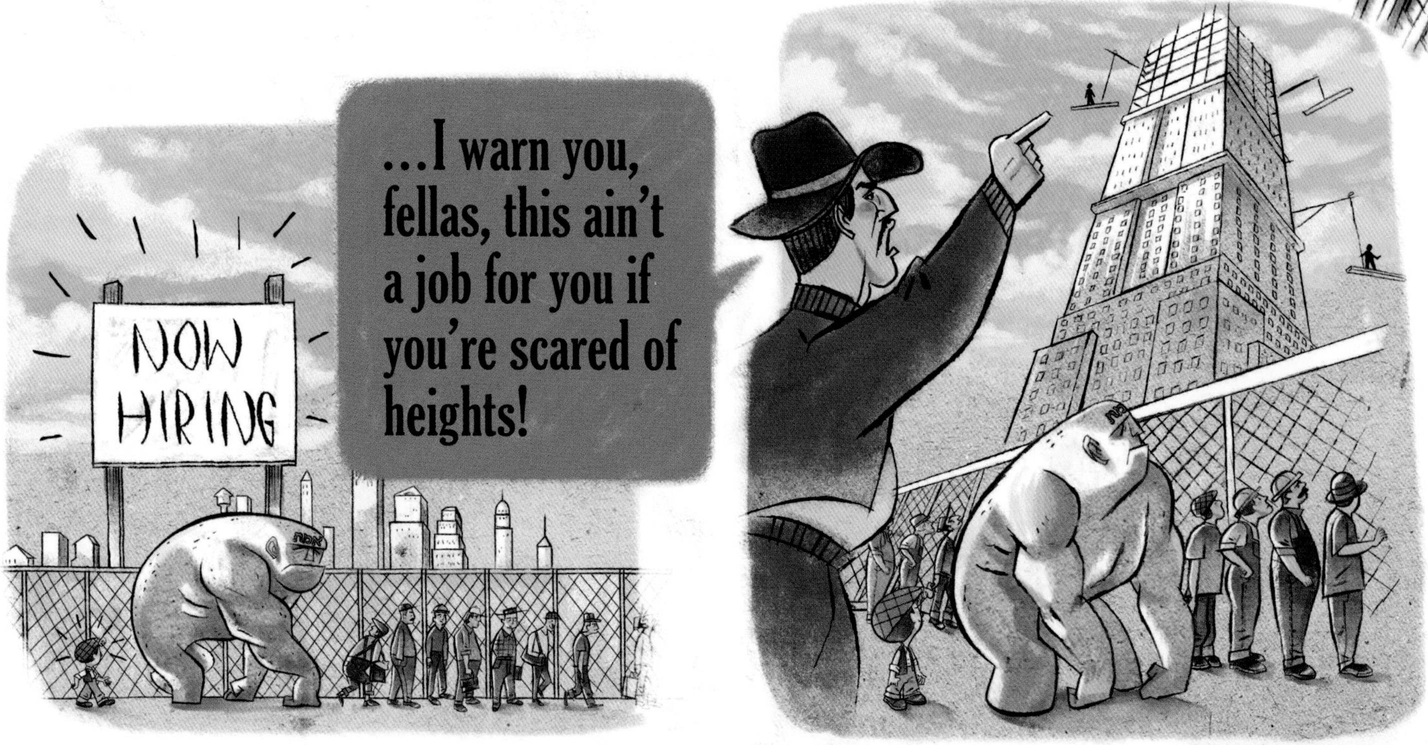
NOW HIRING
…I warn you, fellas, this ain't a job for you if you're scared of heights!

My golem wasn't scared of anything. He could be a construction worker on a skyscraper, for sure!

Unless, of course, everybody else suddenly became very scared of heights!

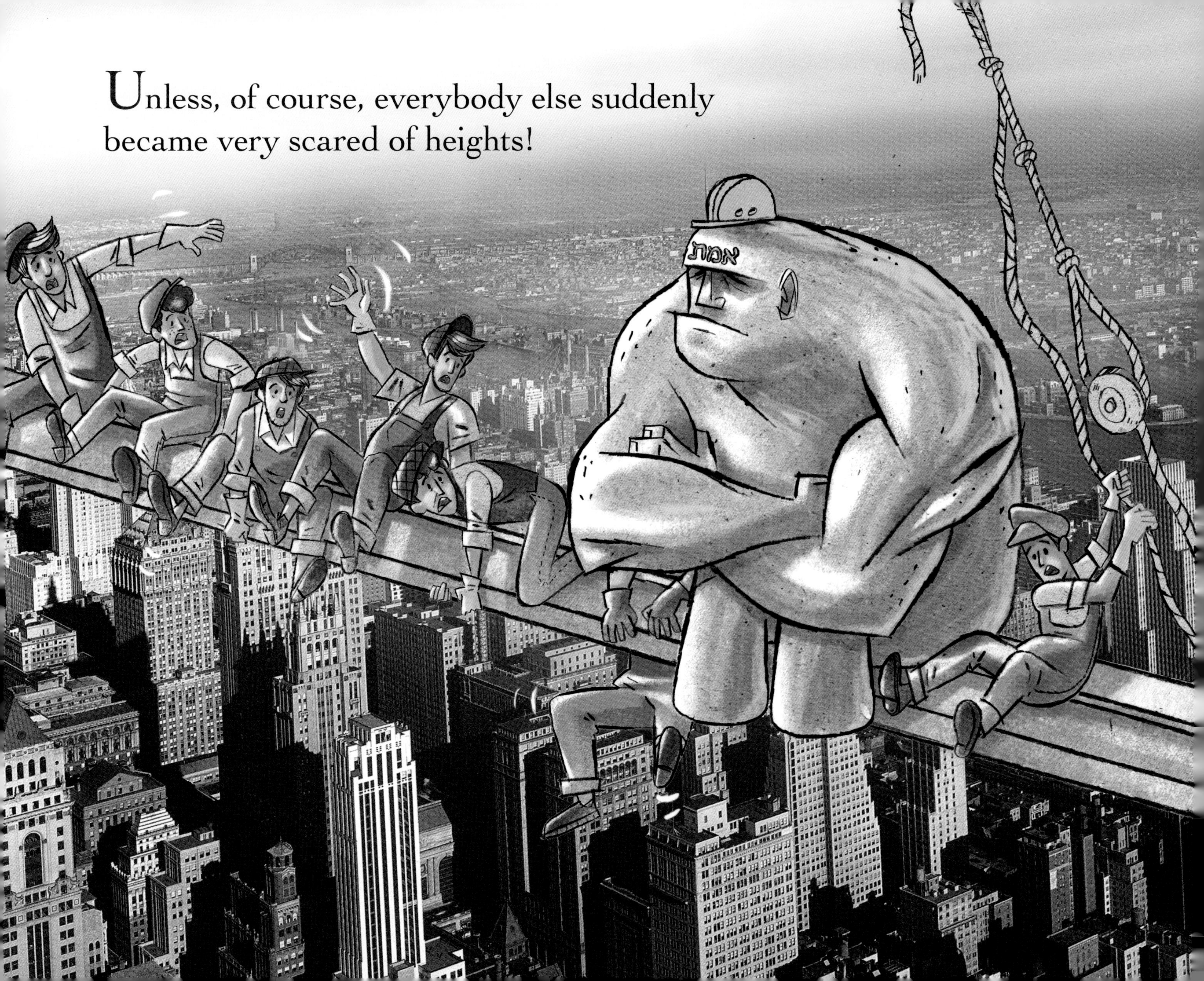
אמת

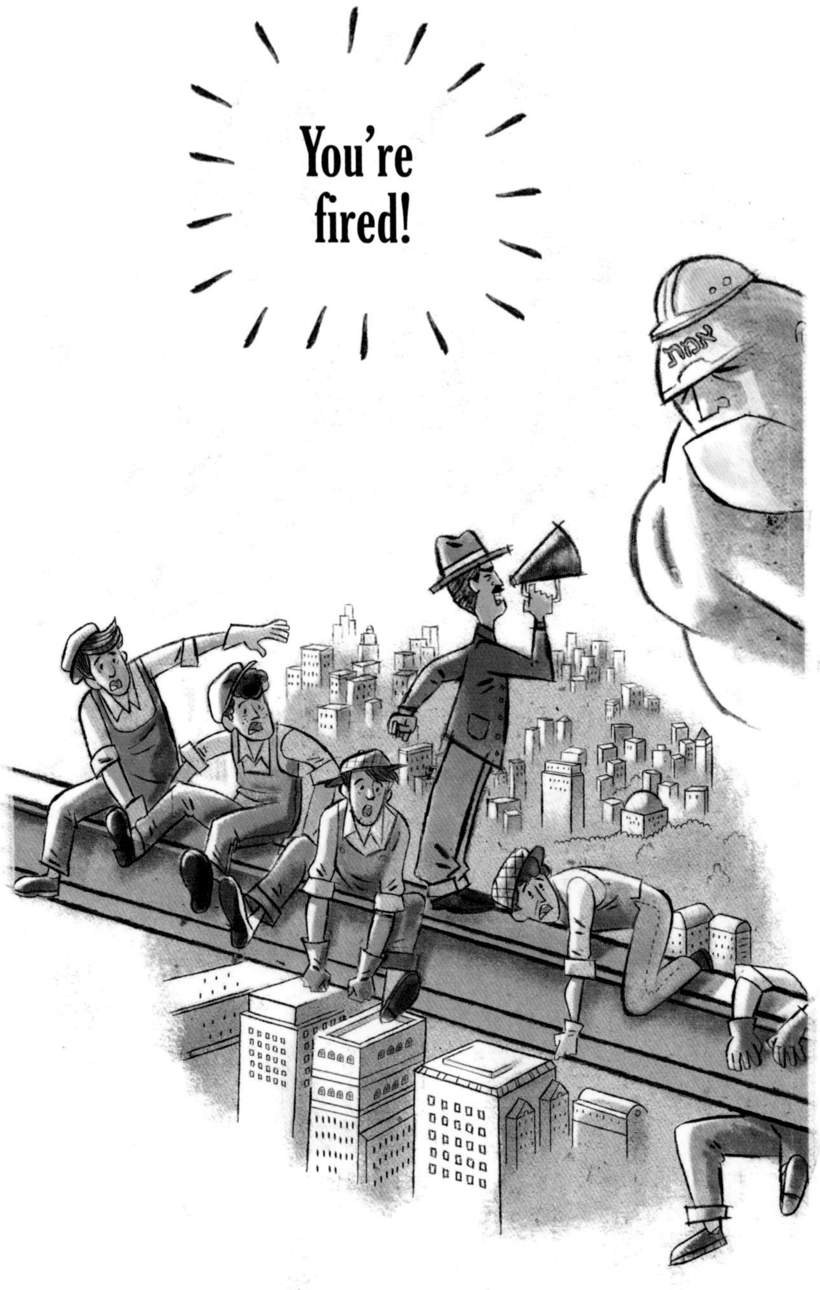
You're fired!
אמת

Now what would my golem do?

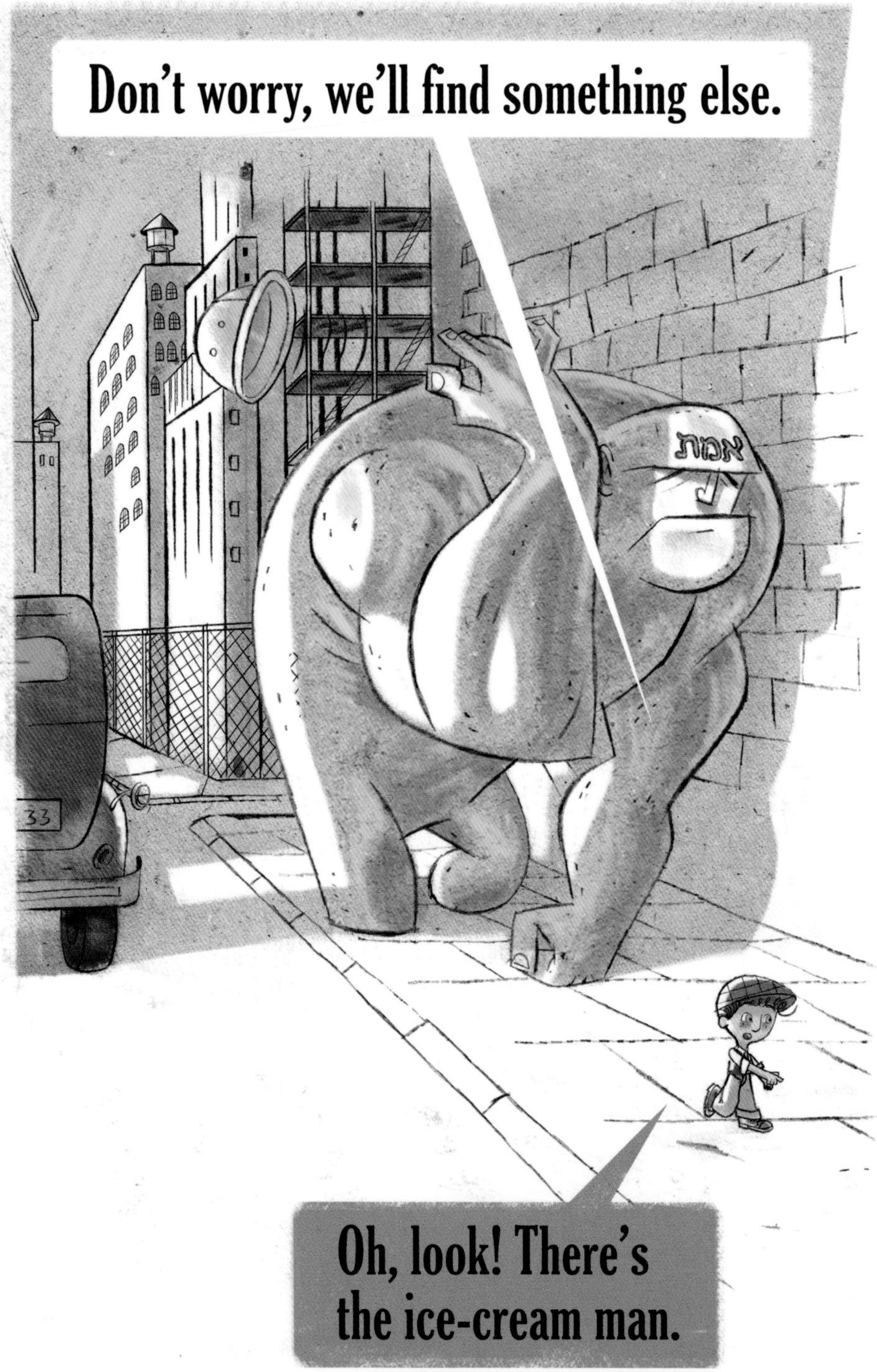
Don't worry, we'll find something else.
אמת
Oh, look! There's the ice-cream man.

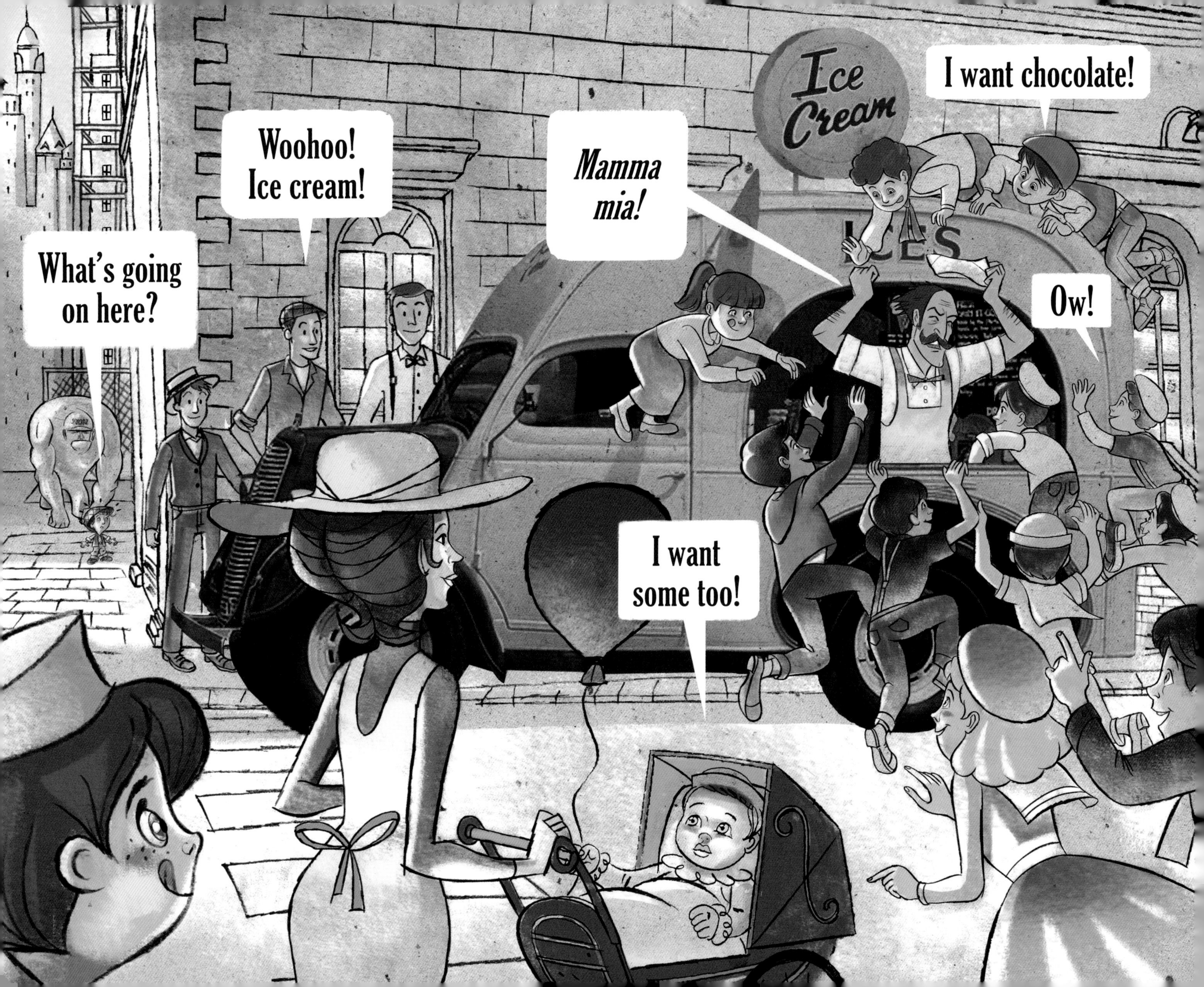
What's going on here?
Woohoo! Ice cream!
Mamma mia!
Ice Cream
I want chocolate!
ICES
Ow!
I want some too!

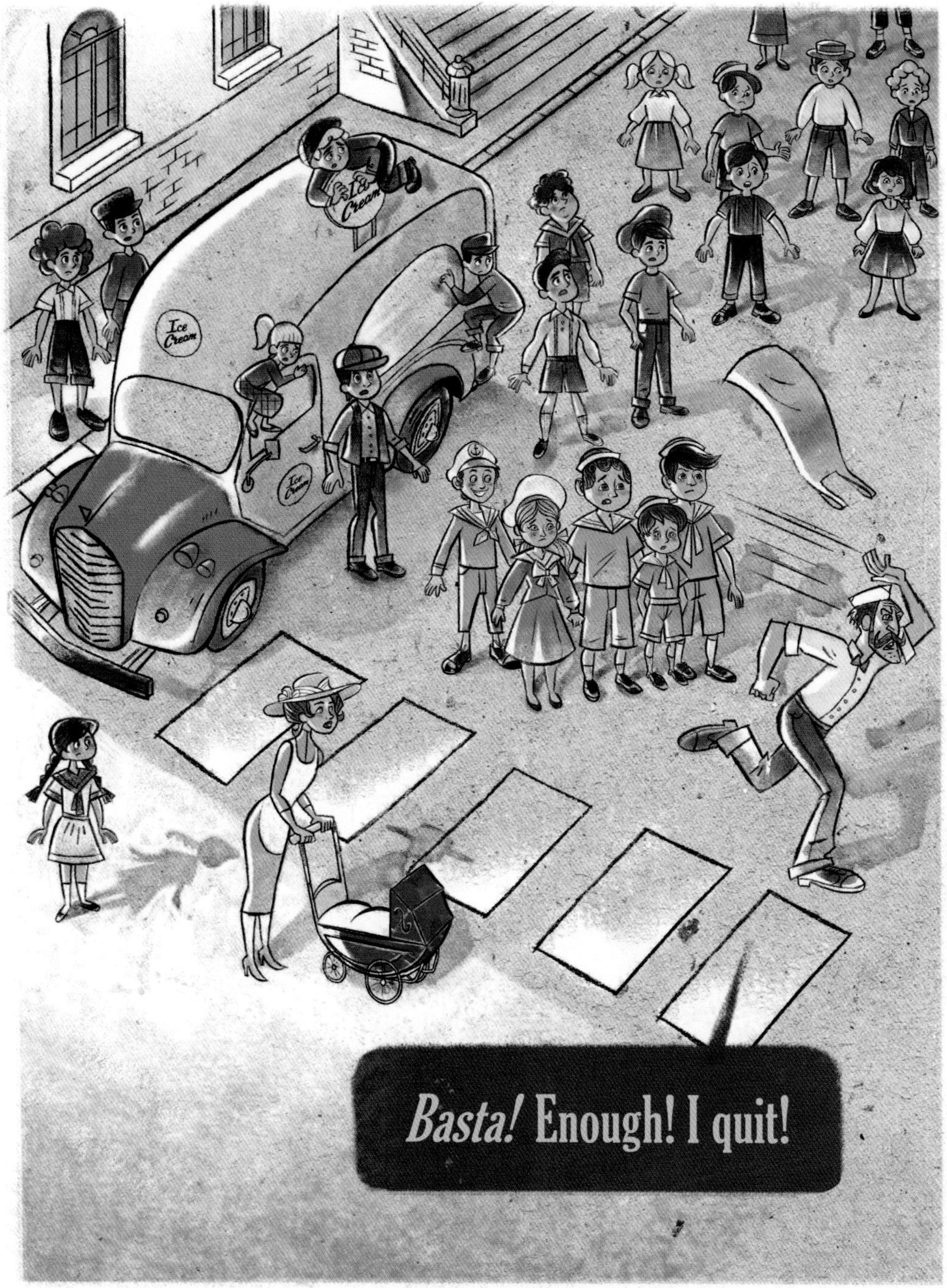
Basta! Enough! I quit!

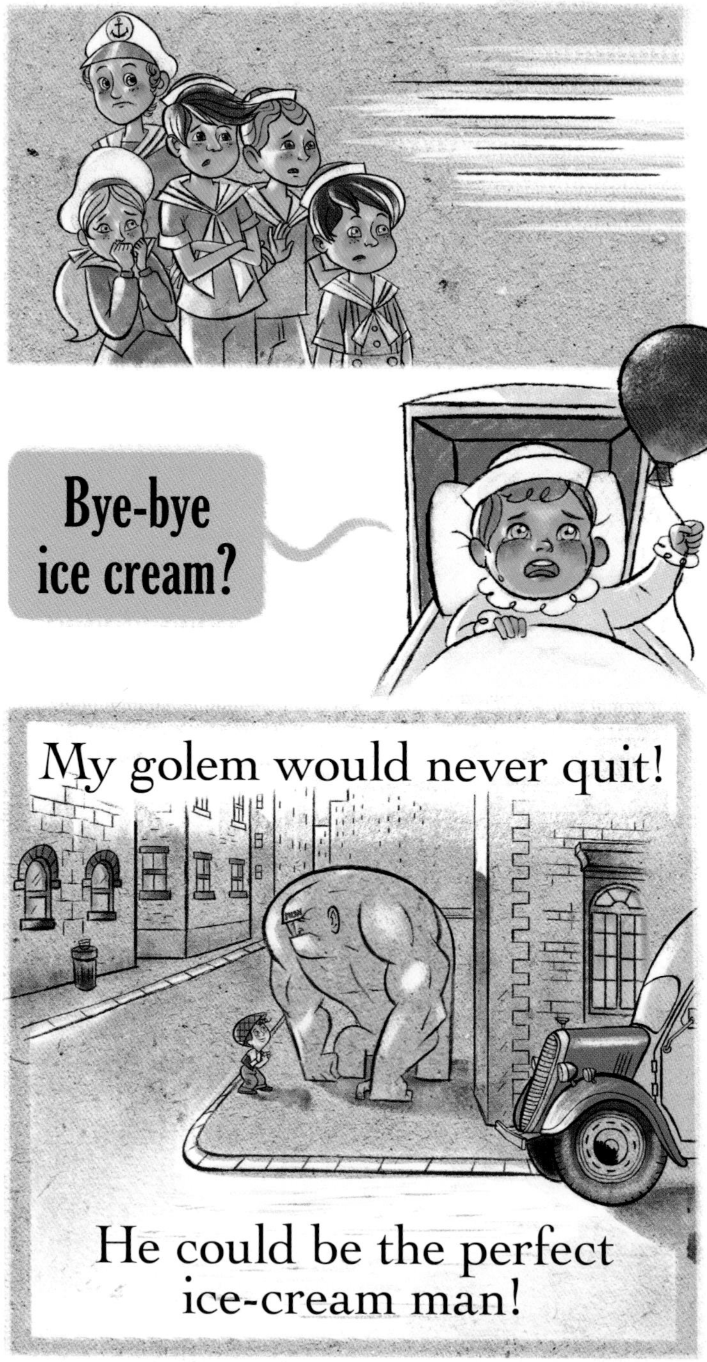
Bye-bye ice cream?
My golem would never quit!
He could be the perfect ice-cream man!

But the kids were so afraid of the new ice-cream man,
they wouldn't come near!

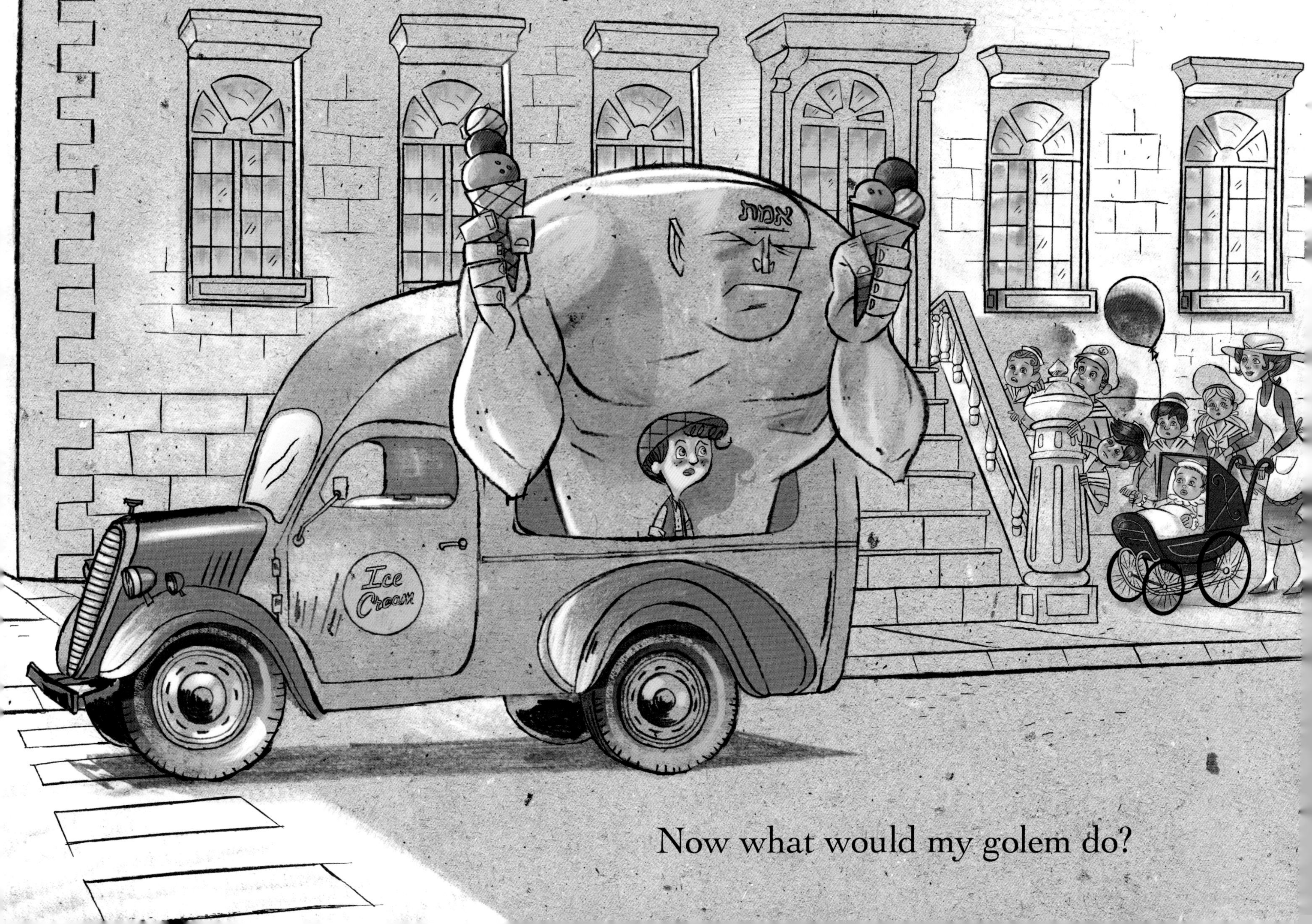
אמת
Ice Cream

Now what would my golem do?

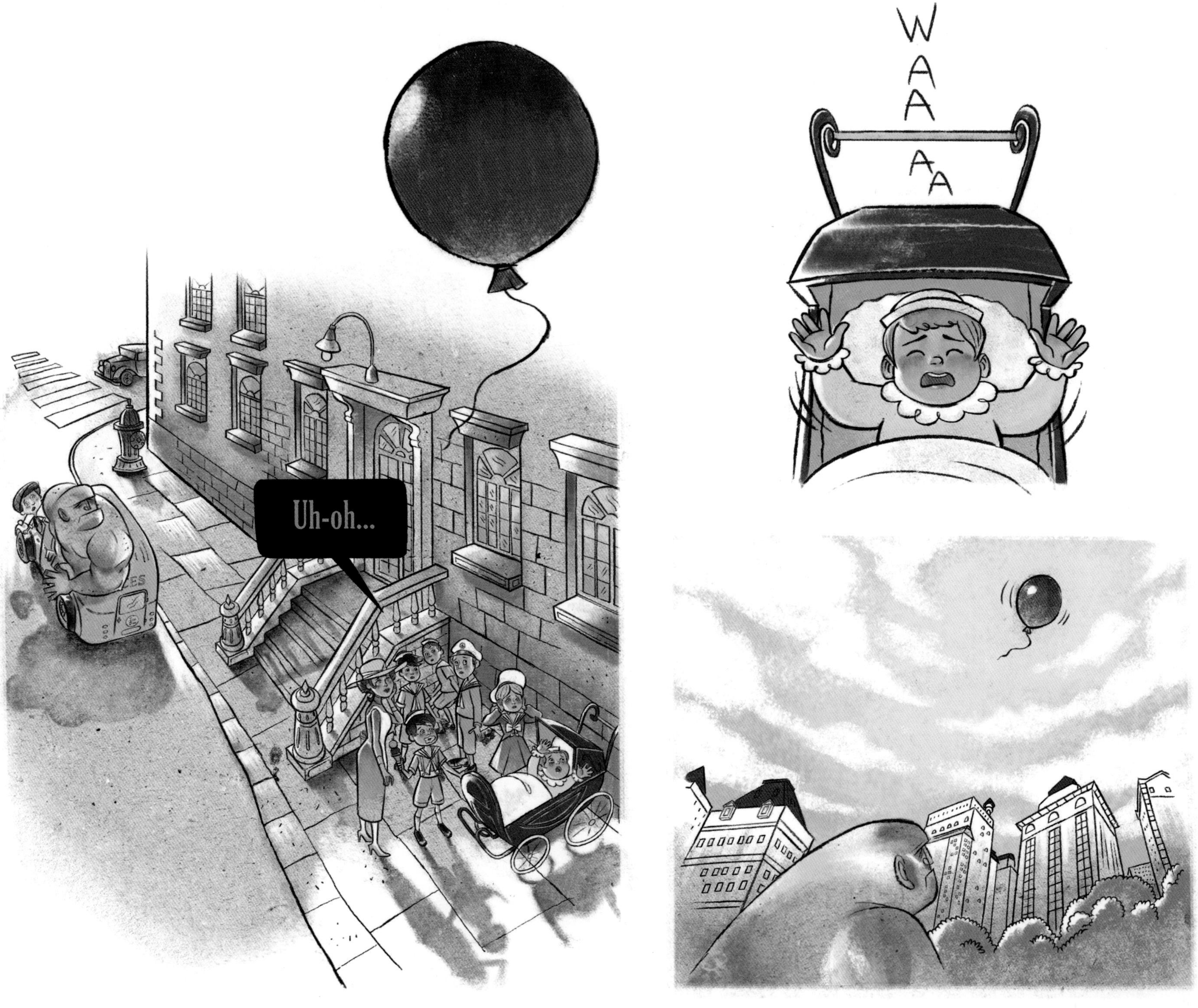
Uh-oh...
WAAAA

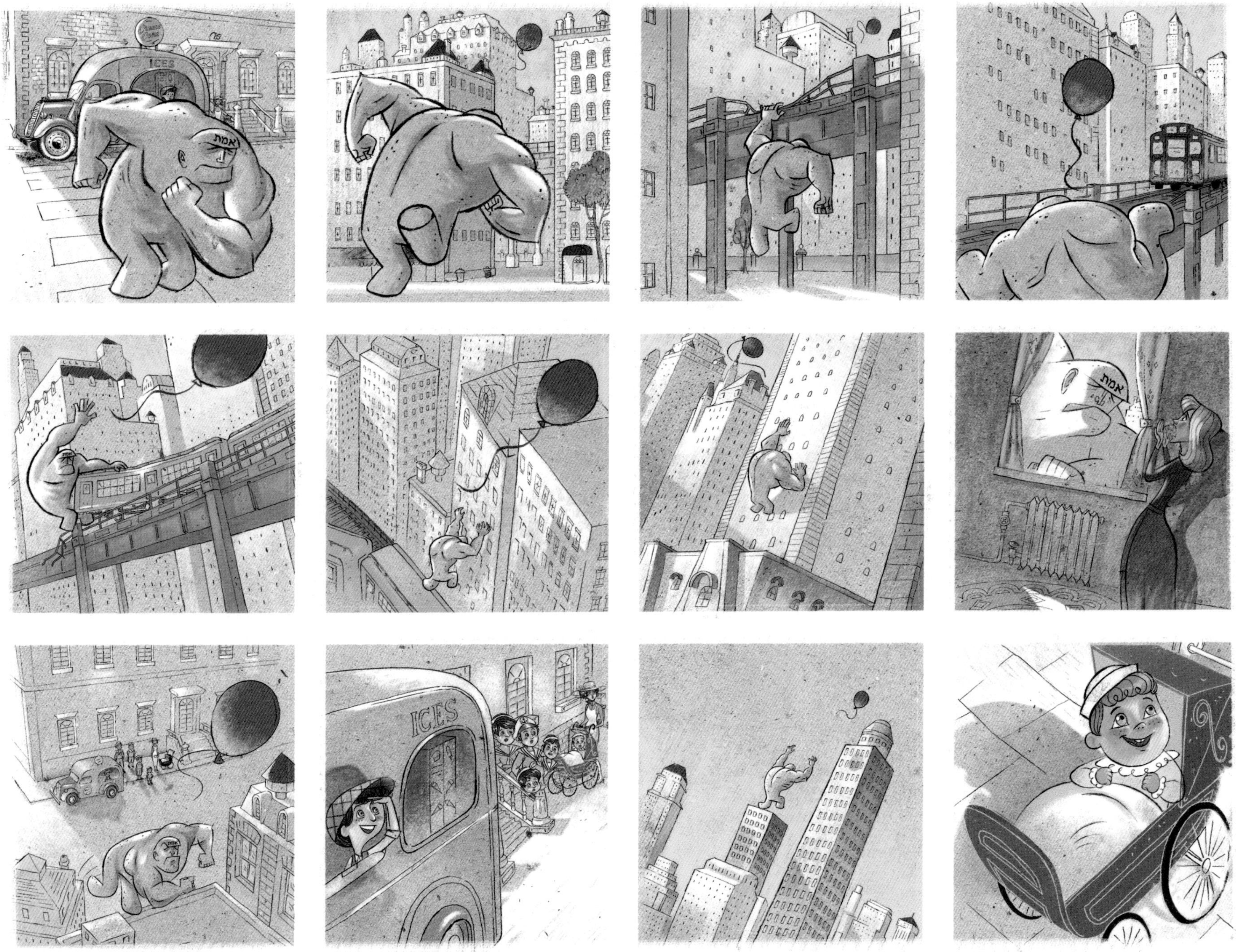
ICES
אמת

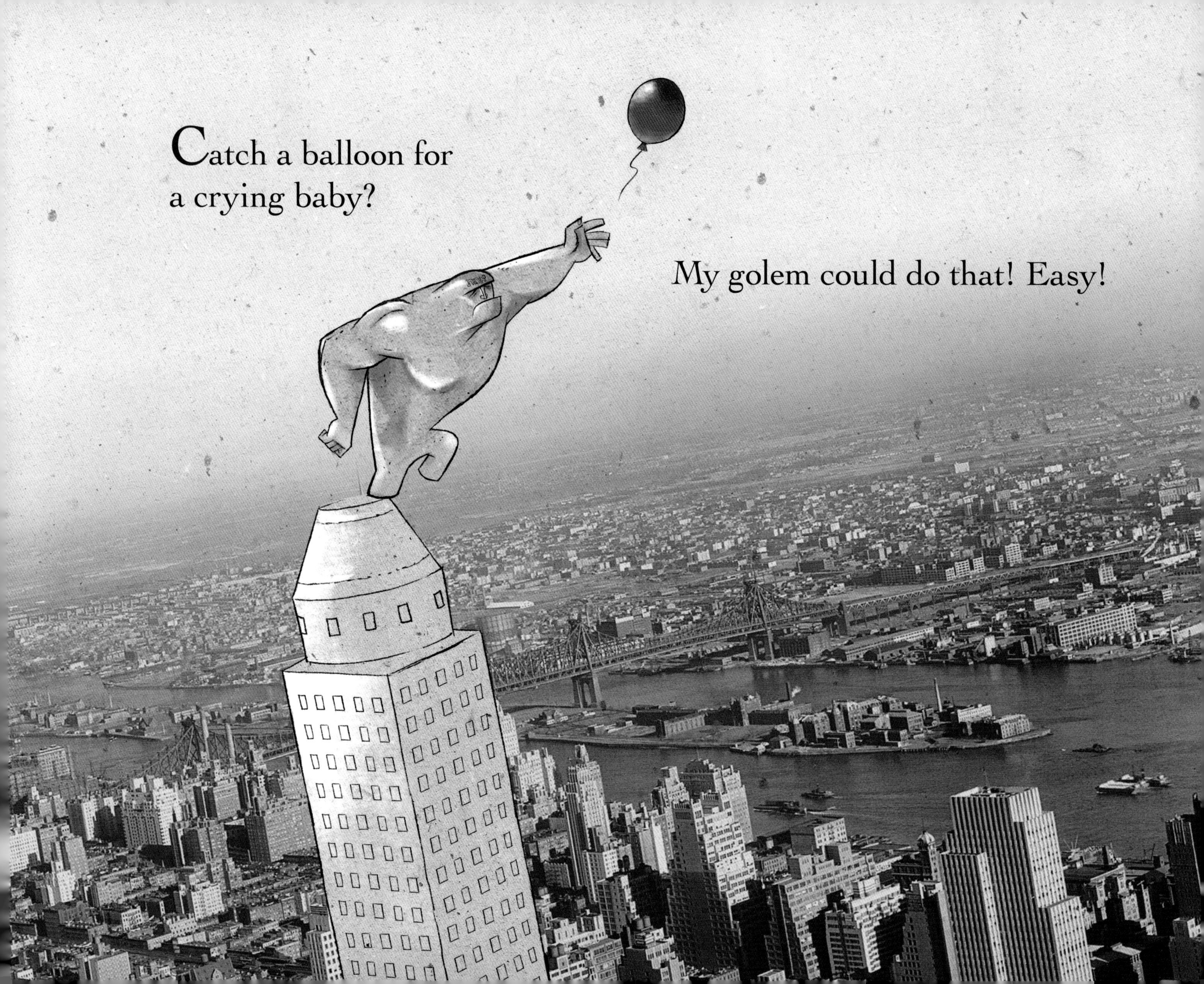

Catch a balloon for
a crying baby?

My golem could do that! Easy!

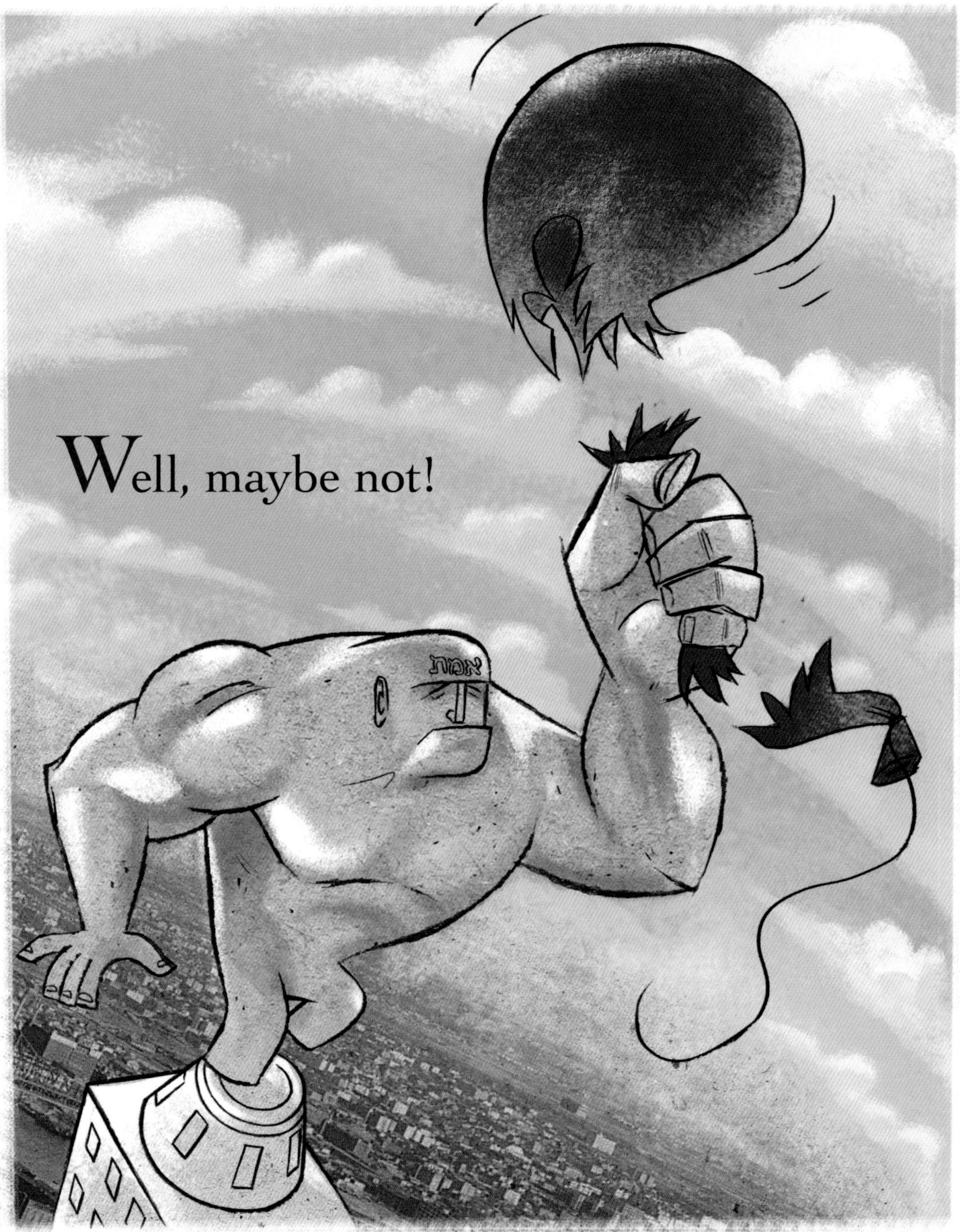
אמת

Well, maybe not!

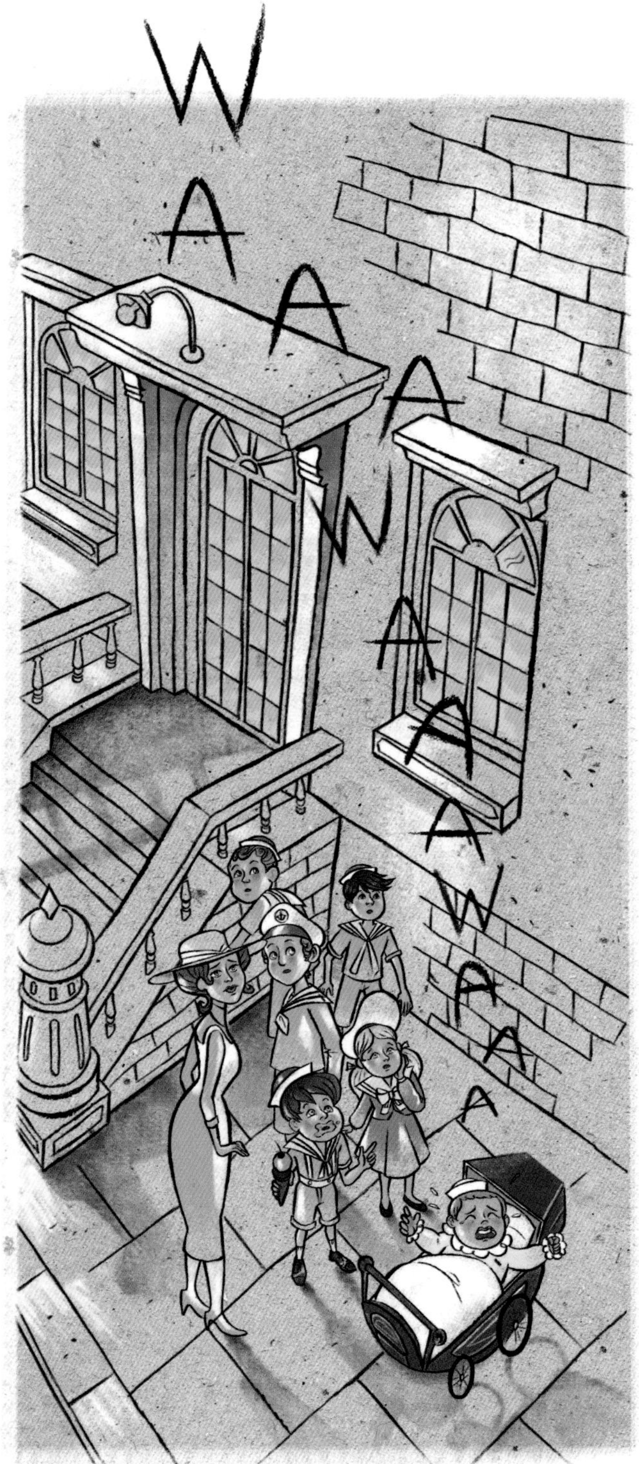
WAAAWAAAWAAA

Now what would my golem do?

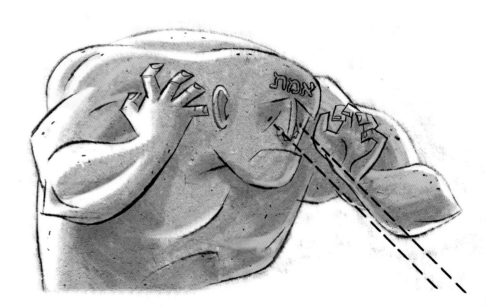

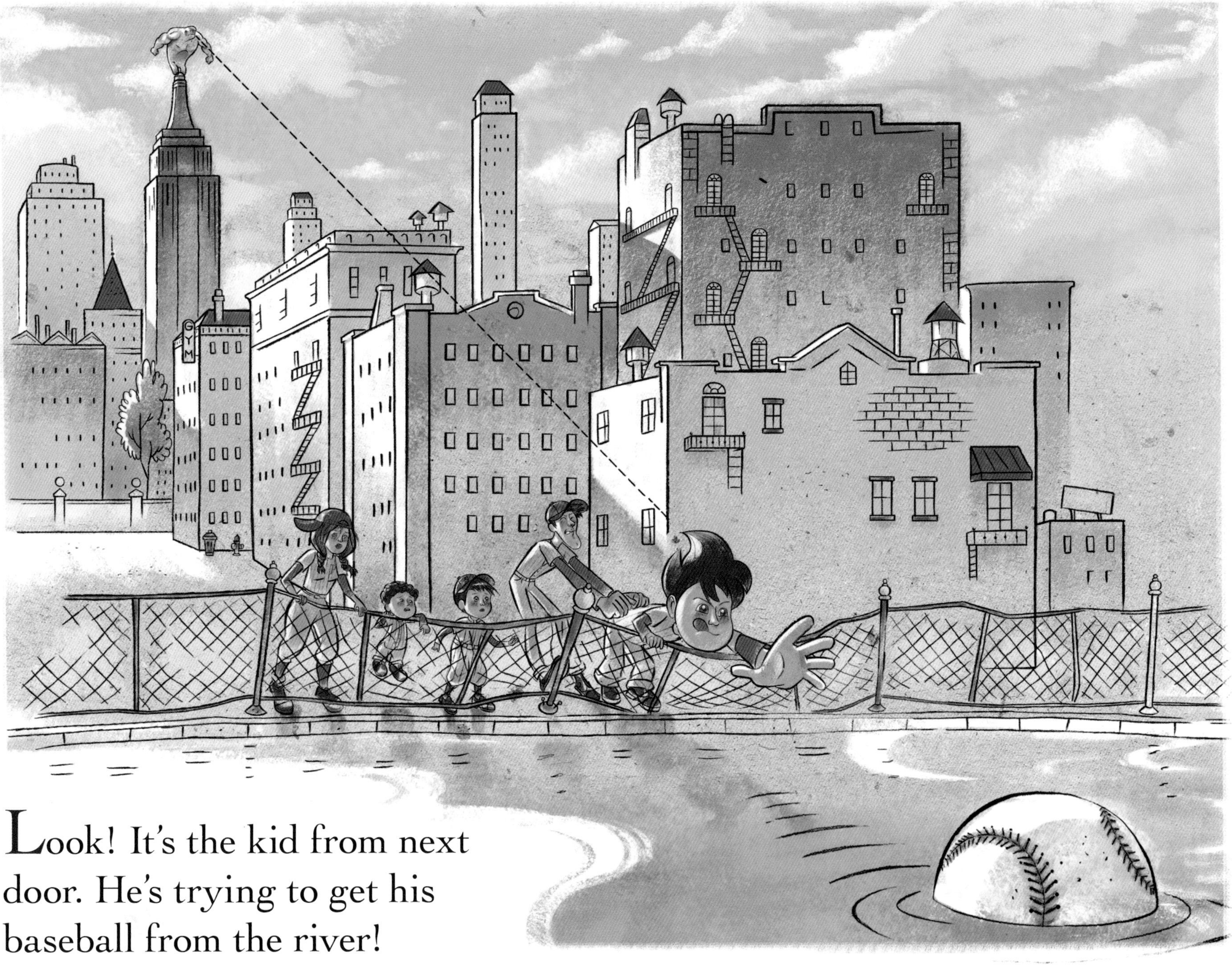
GYM

Look! It's the kid from next door. He's trying to get his baseball from the river!

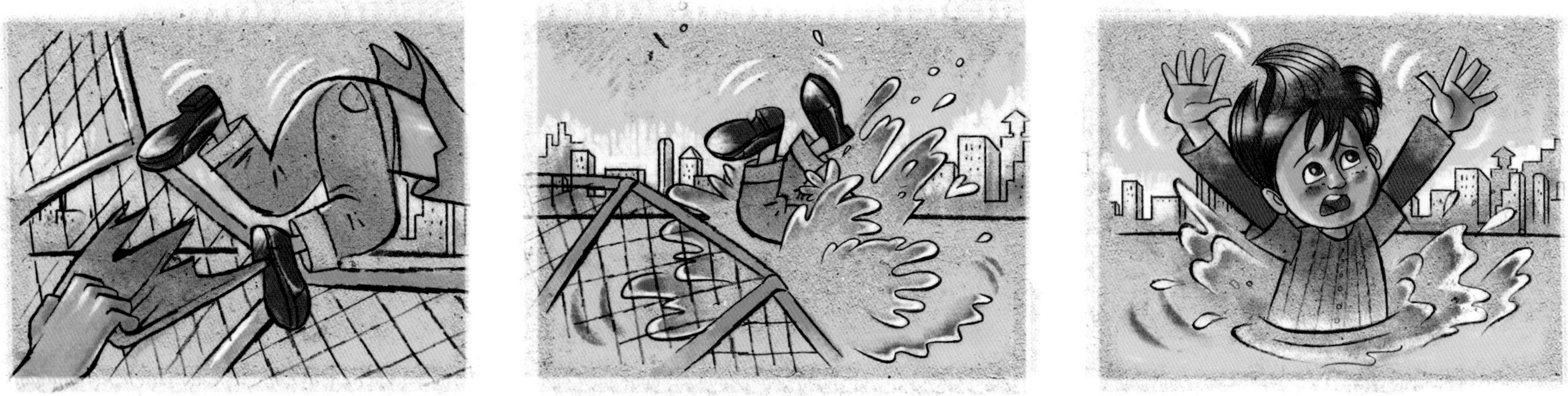

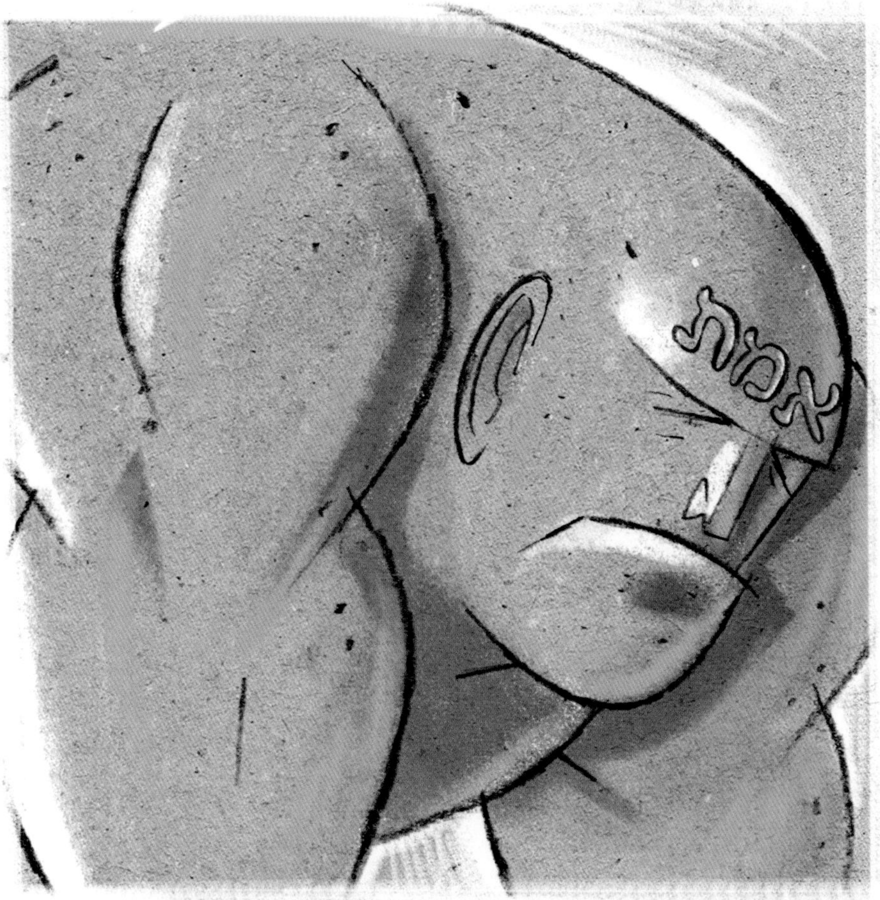
אמת

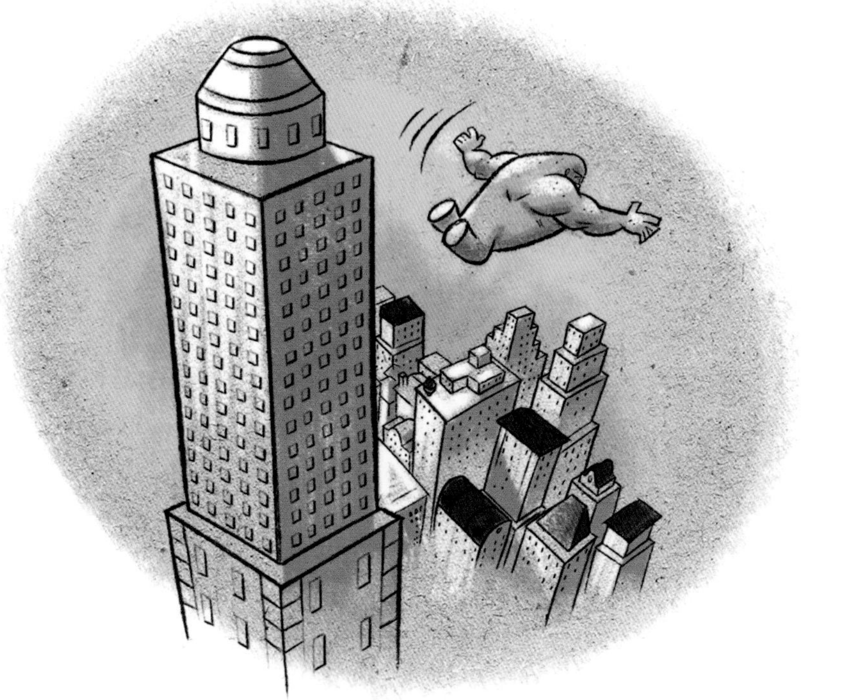

My golem would always come to the rescue. He could be a superhero!

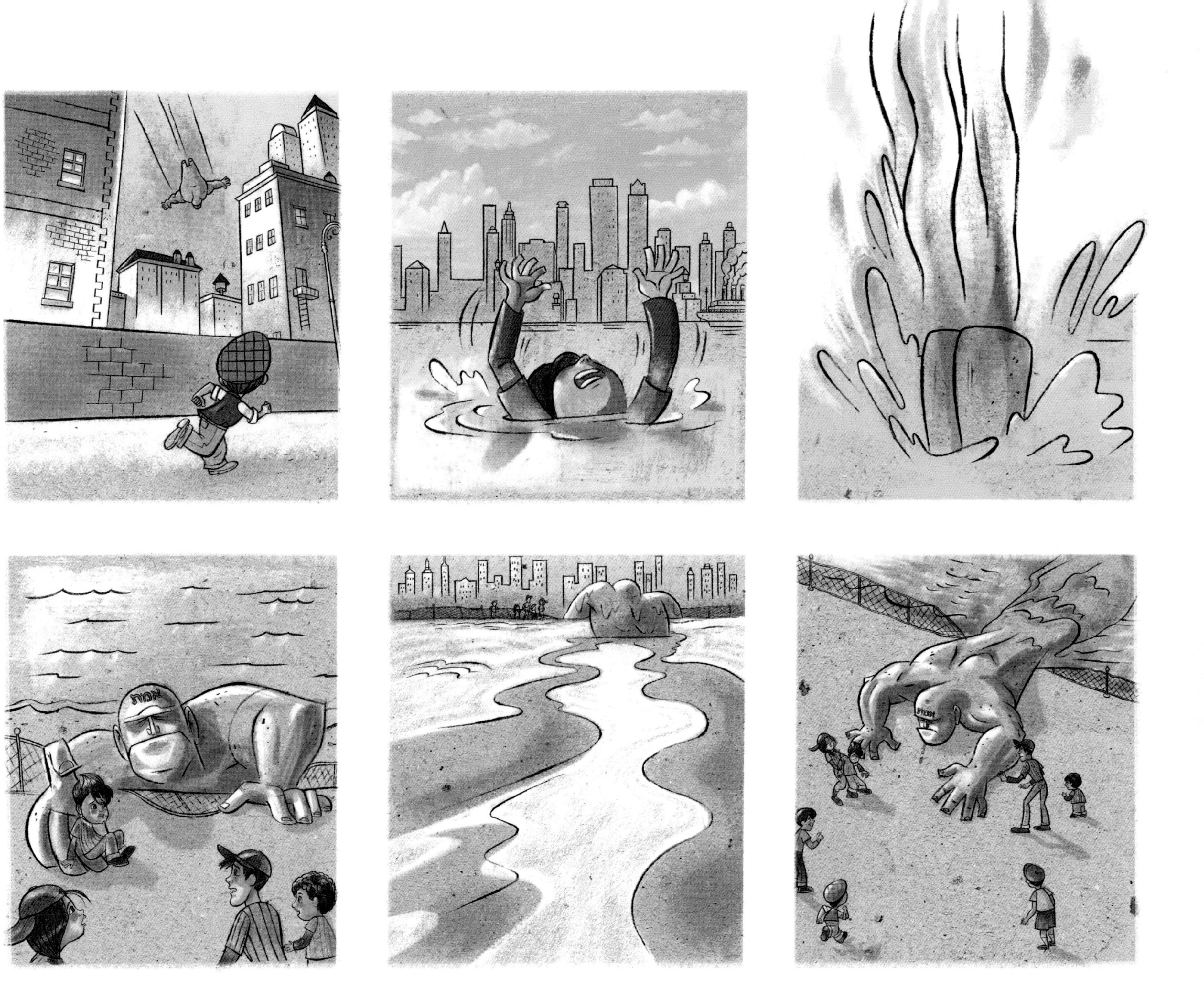

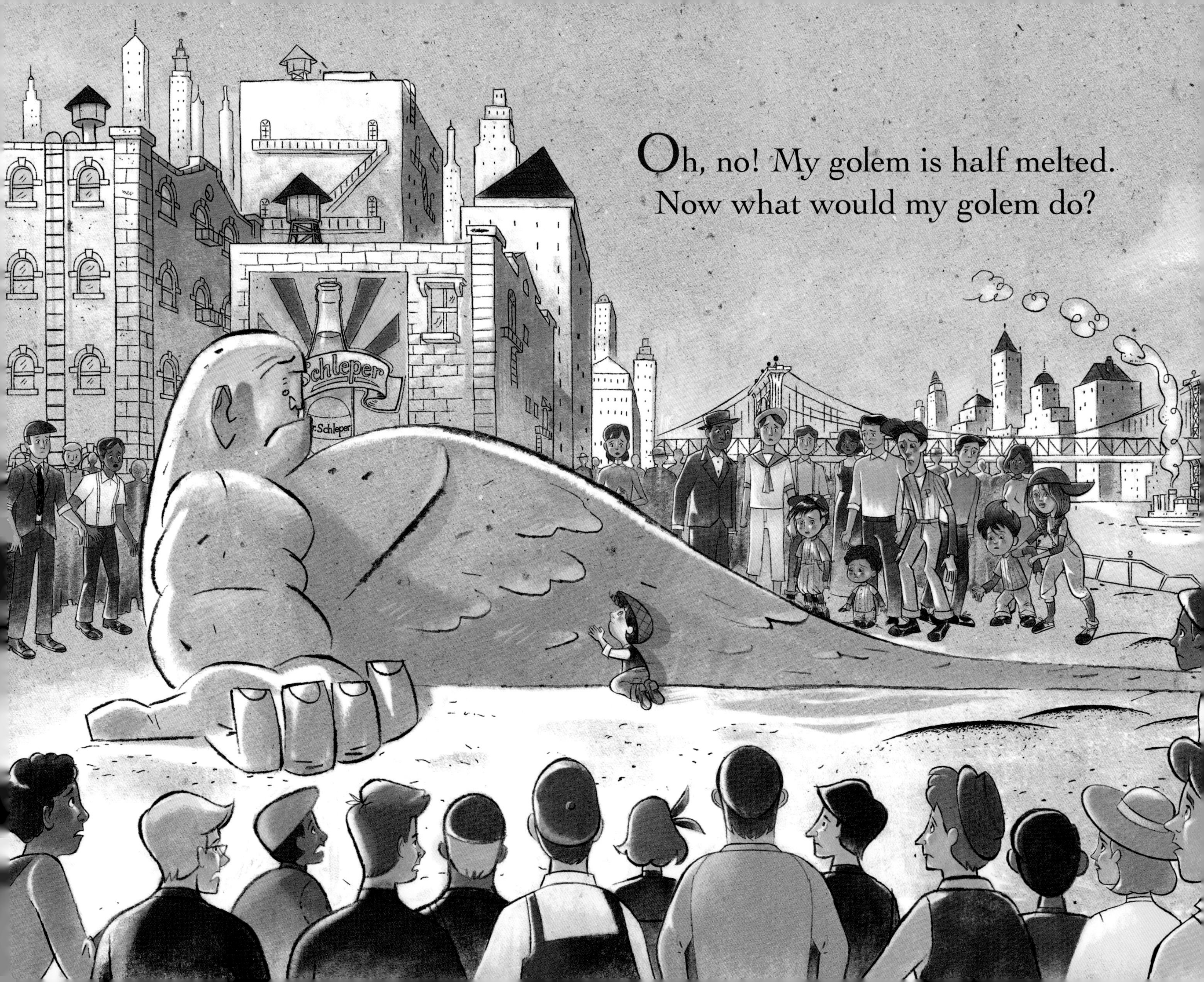

Oh, no! My golem is half melted.
Now what would my golem do?

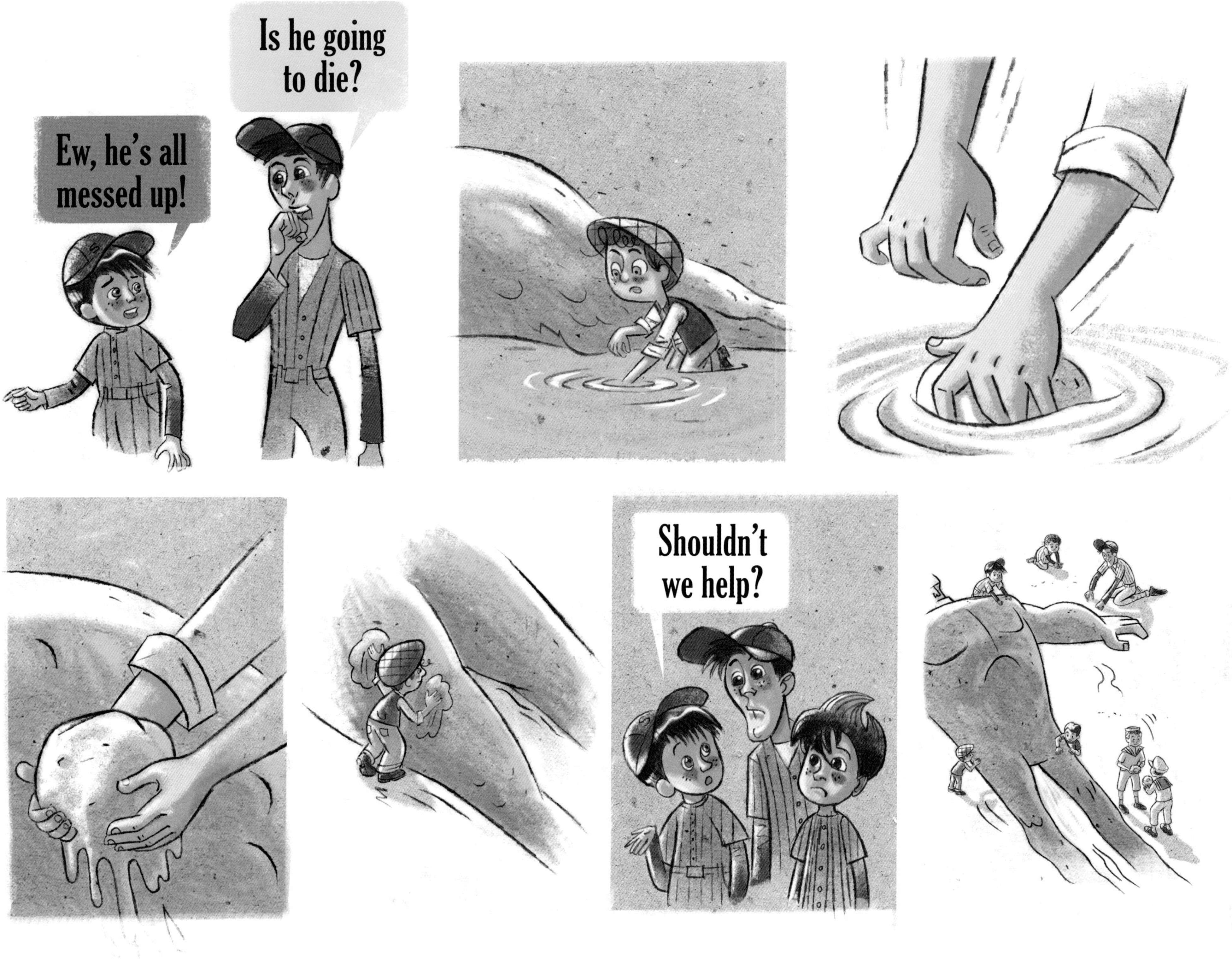
Ew, he's all messed up!
Is he going to die?
Shouldn't we help?

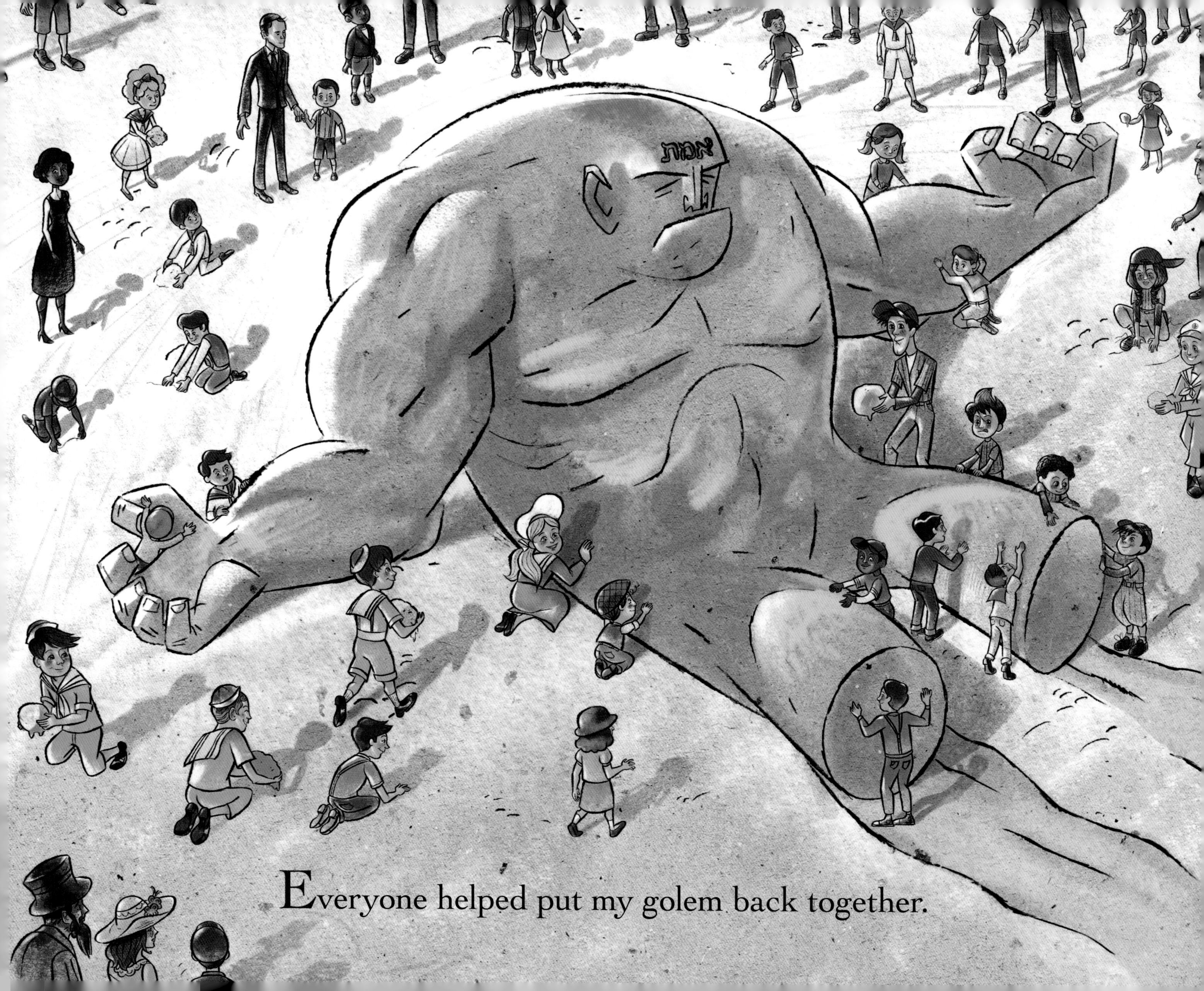
אמת

Everyone helped put my golem back together.

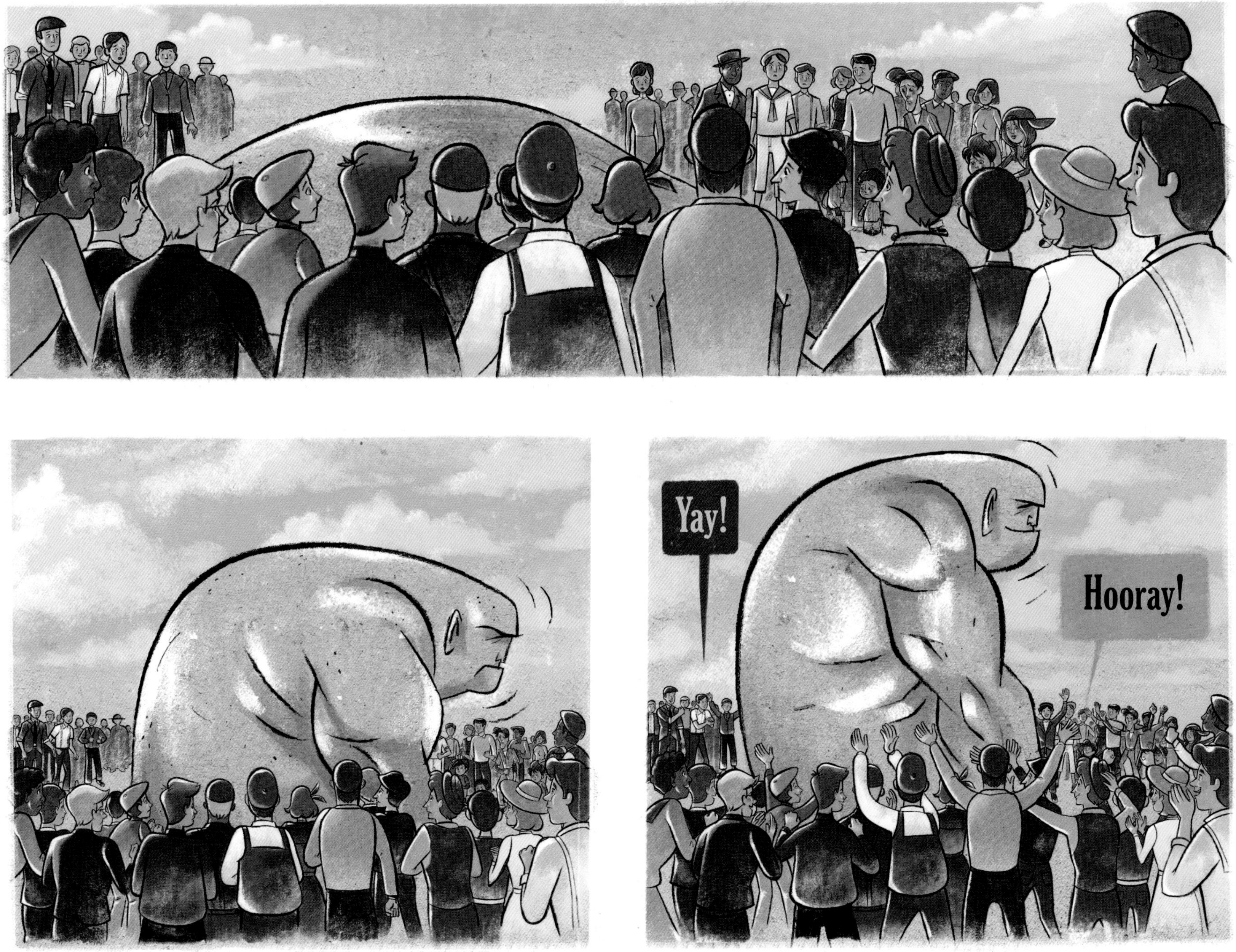
Yay!
Hooray!

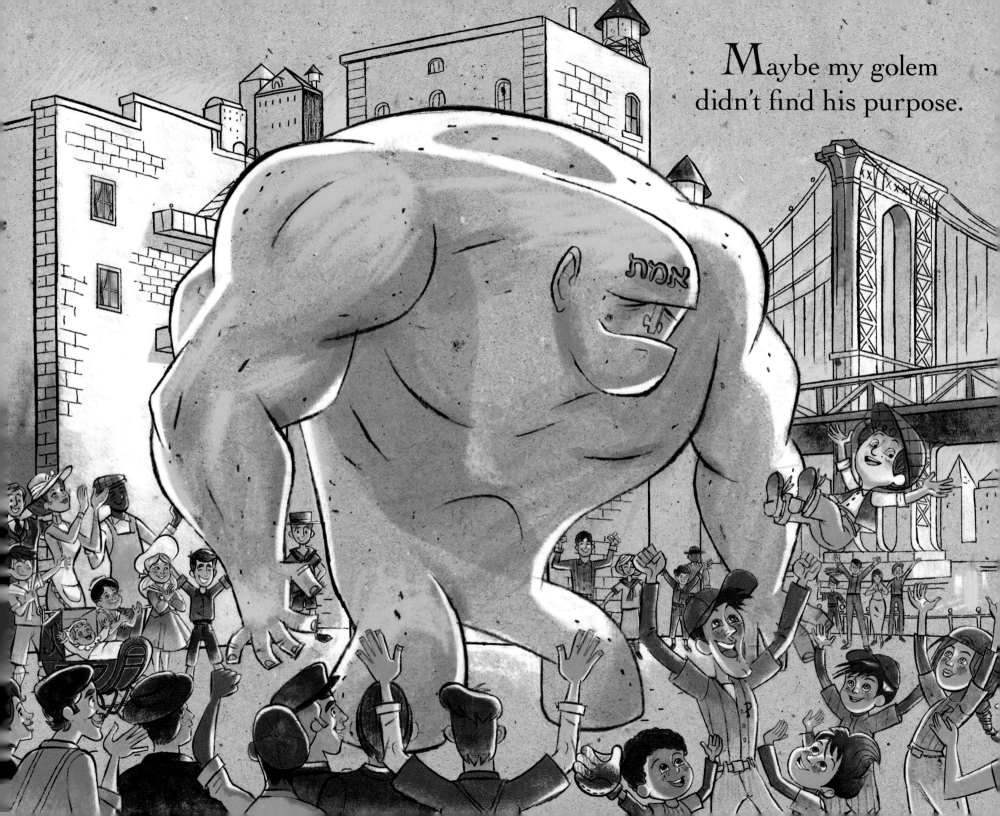

Maybe my golem
didn't find his purpose.

But we found friends, for sure.
And that was more important than anything else!

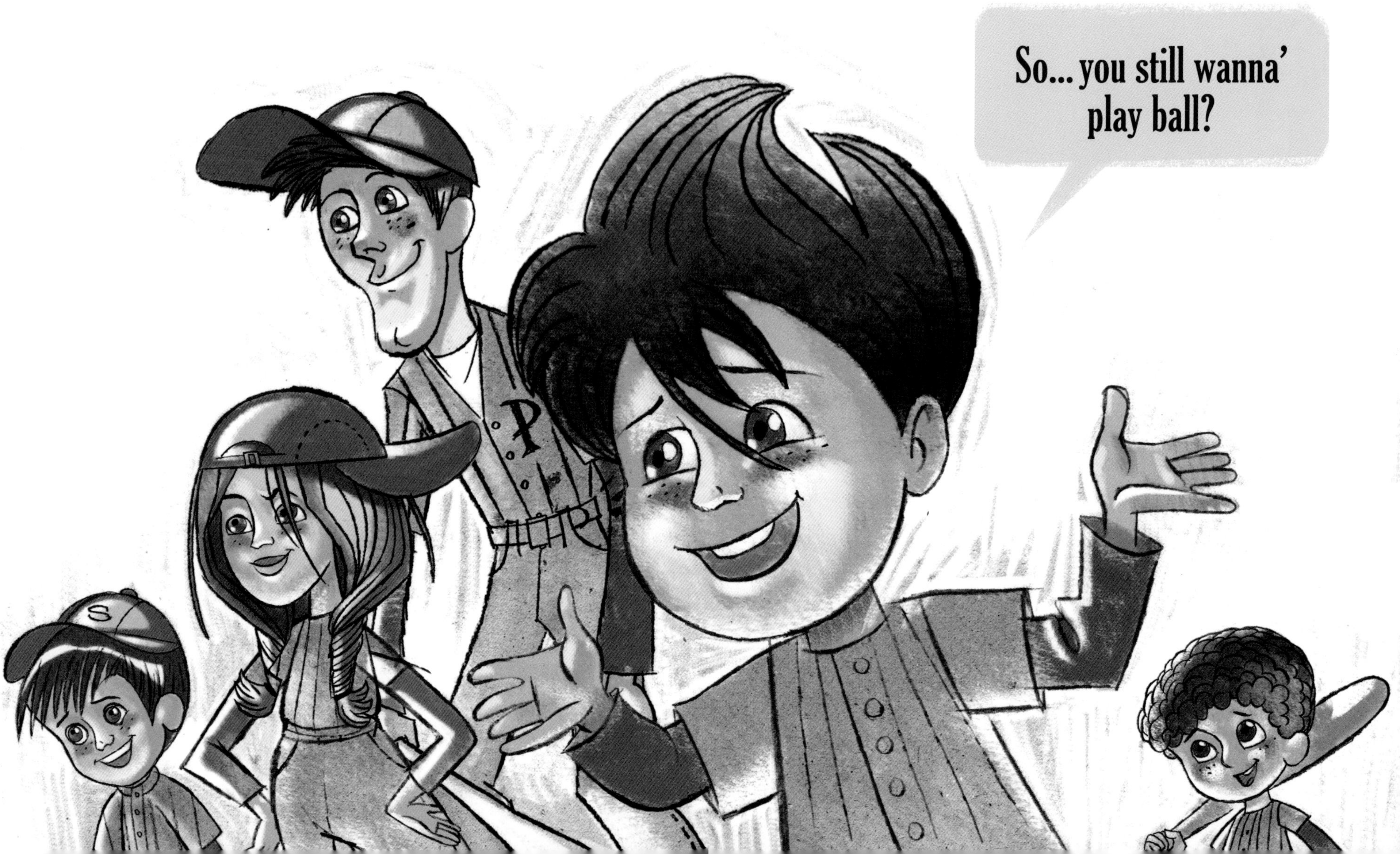
So... you still wanna' play ball?

Play ball?

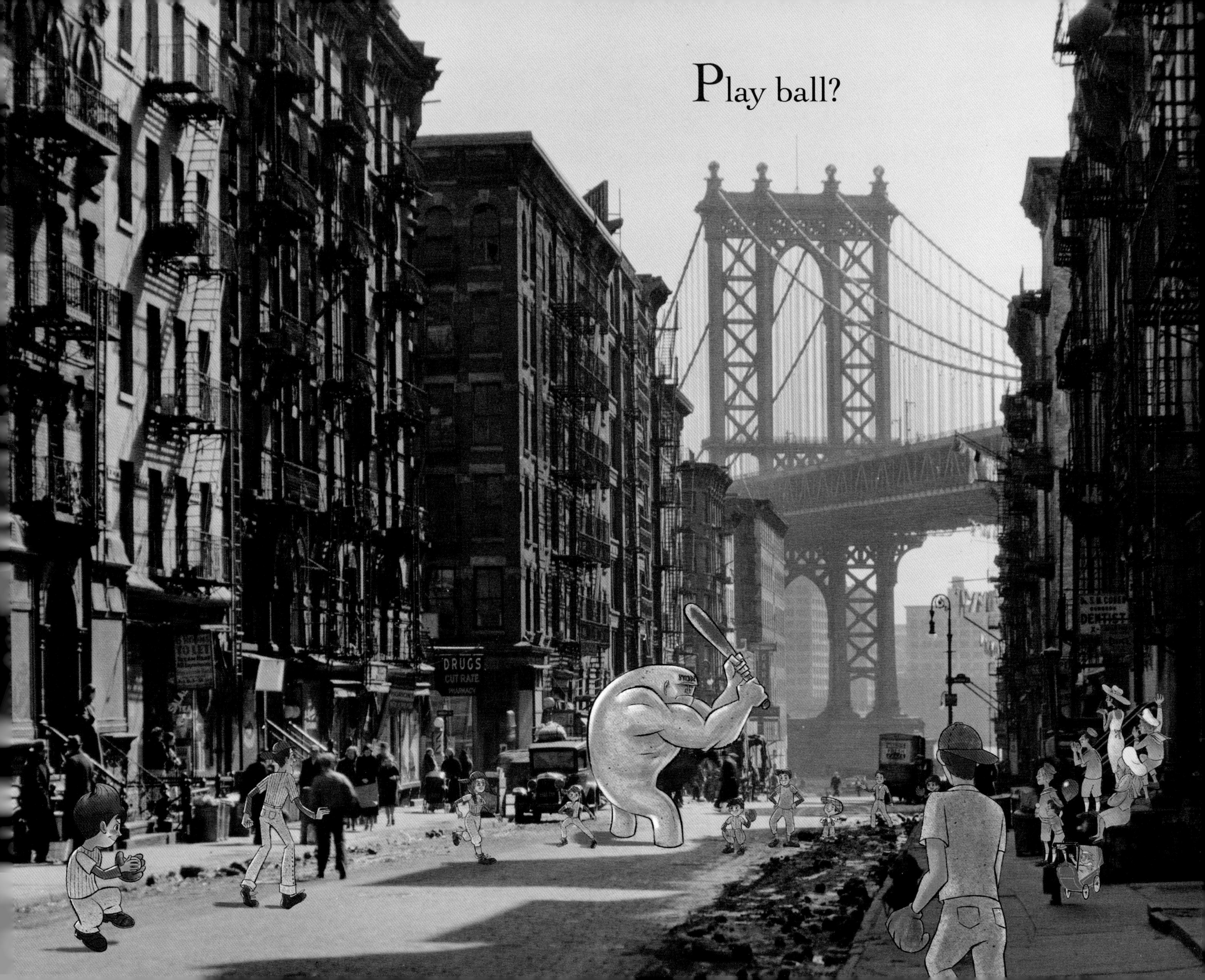
DRUGS
CUT RATE
DENTIST

Sure! My golem could do that,

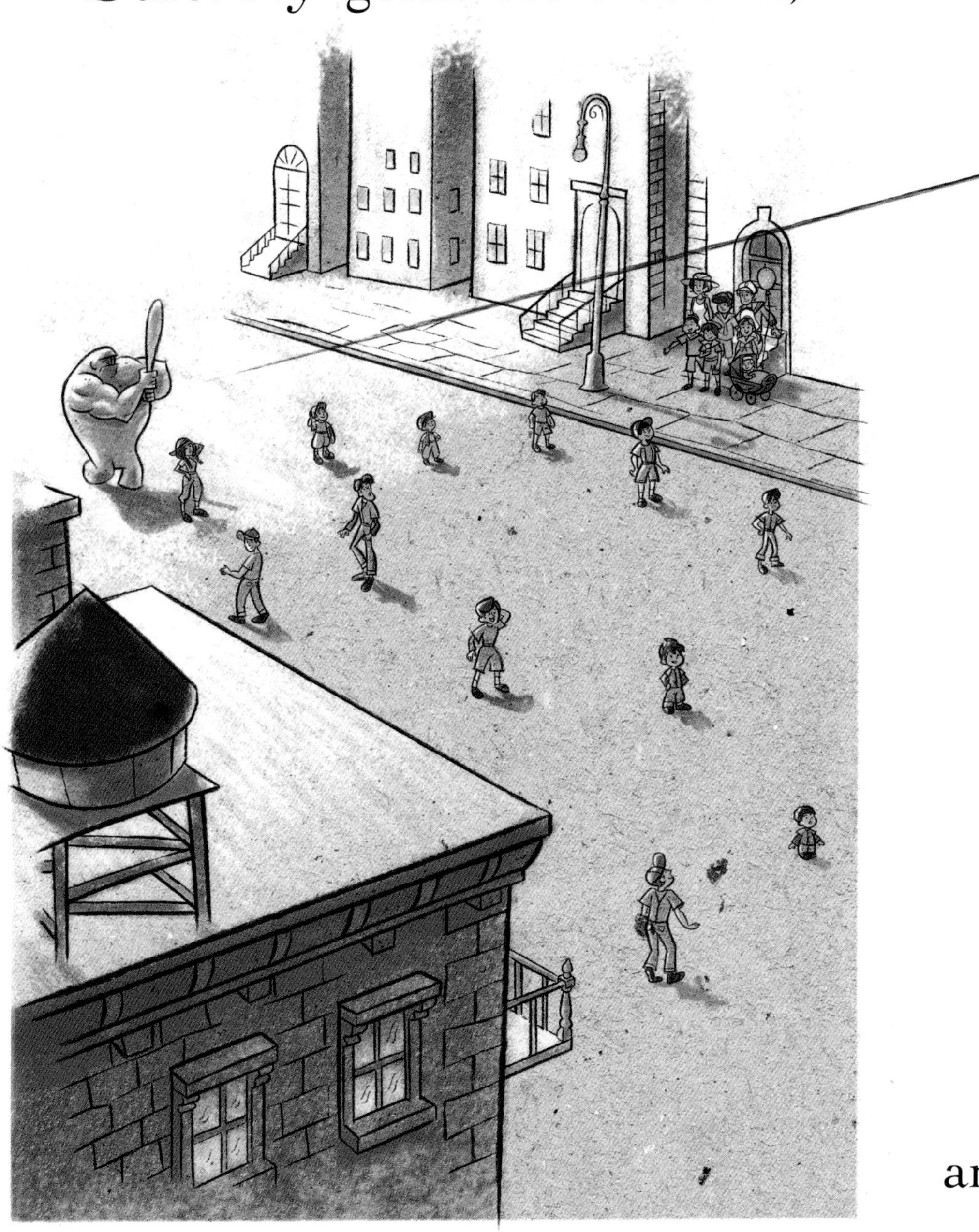

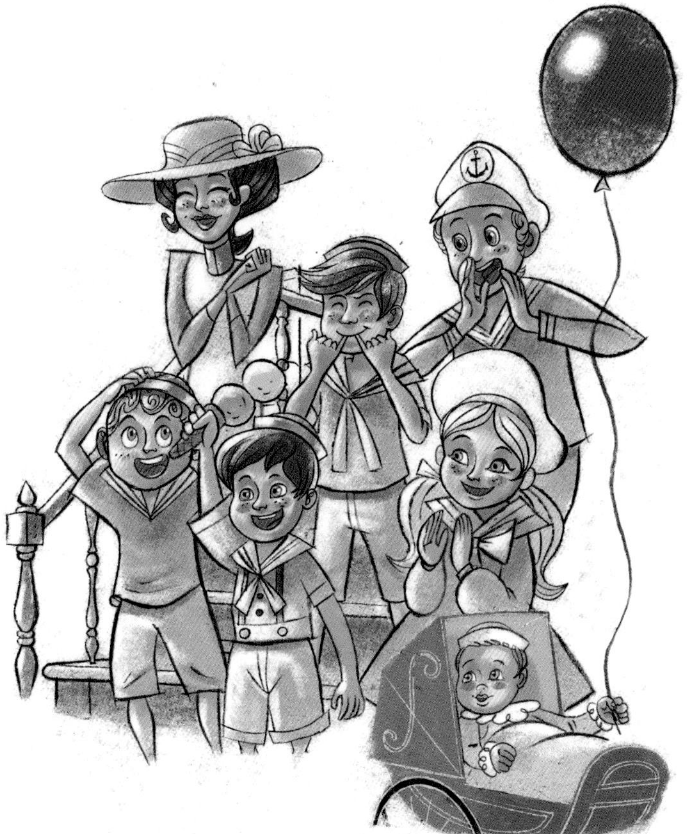

and knock the ball out of the park!

Waaaaaaaaaaaaaaaaaaaaaaaaaaaaaaaaaaaaaaaaaaaaaaaaaaaaaaaay out!

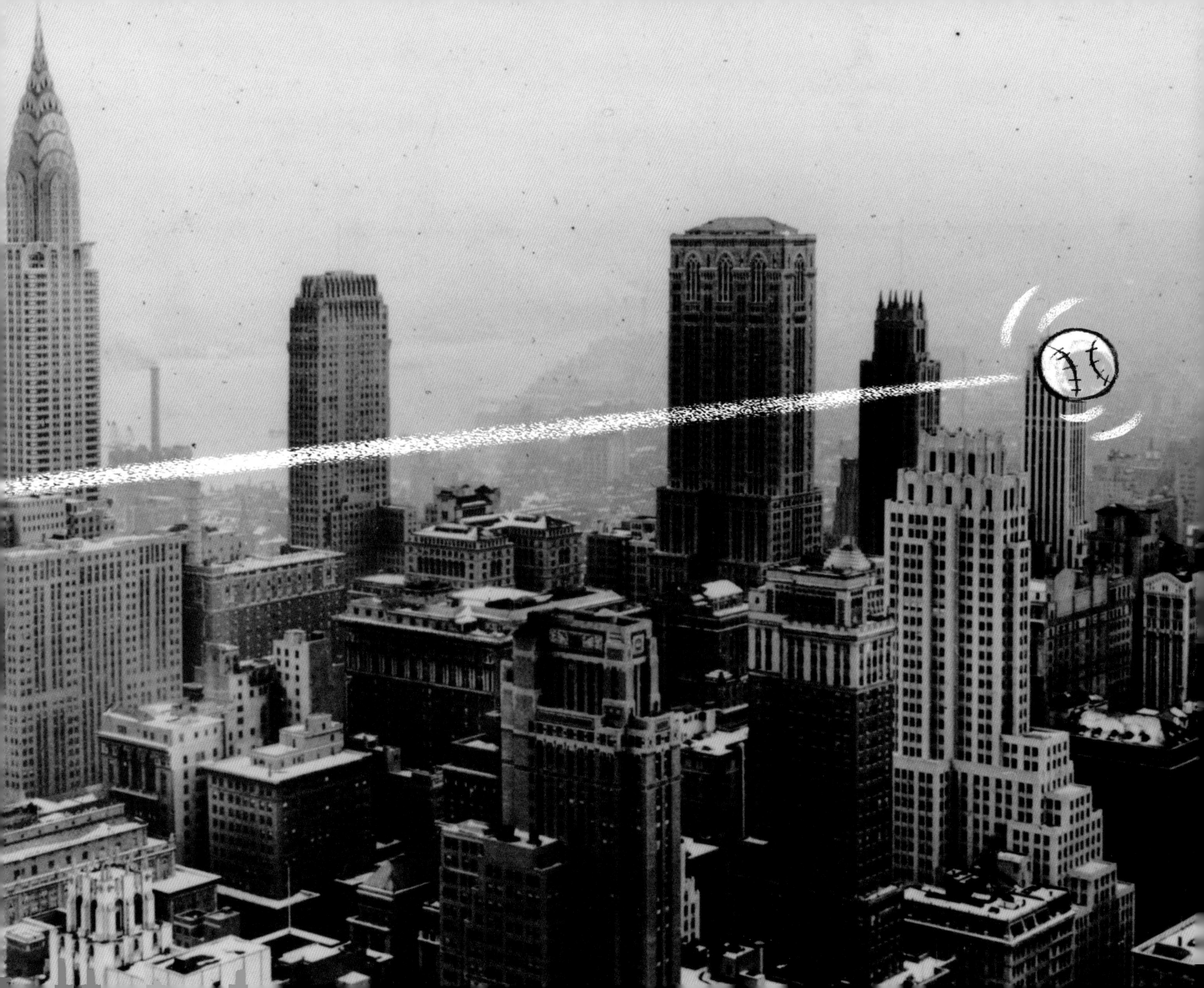

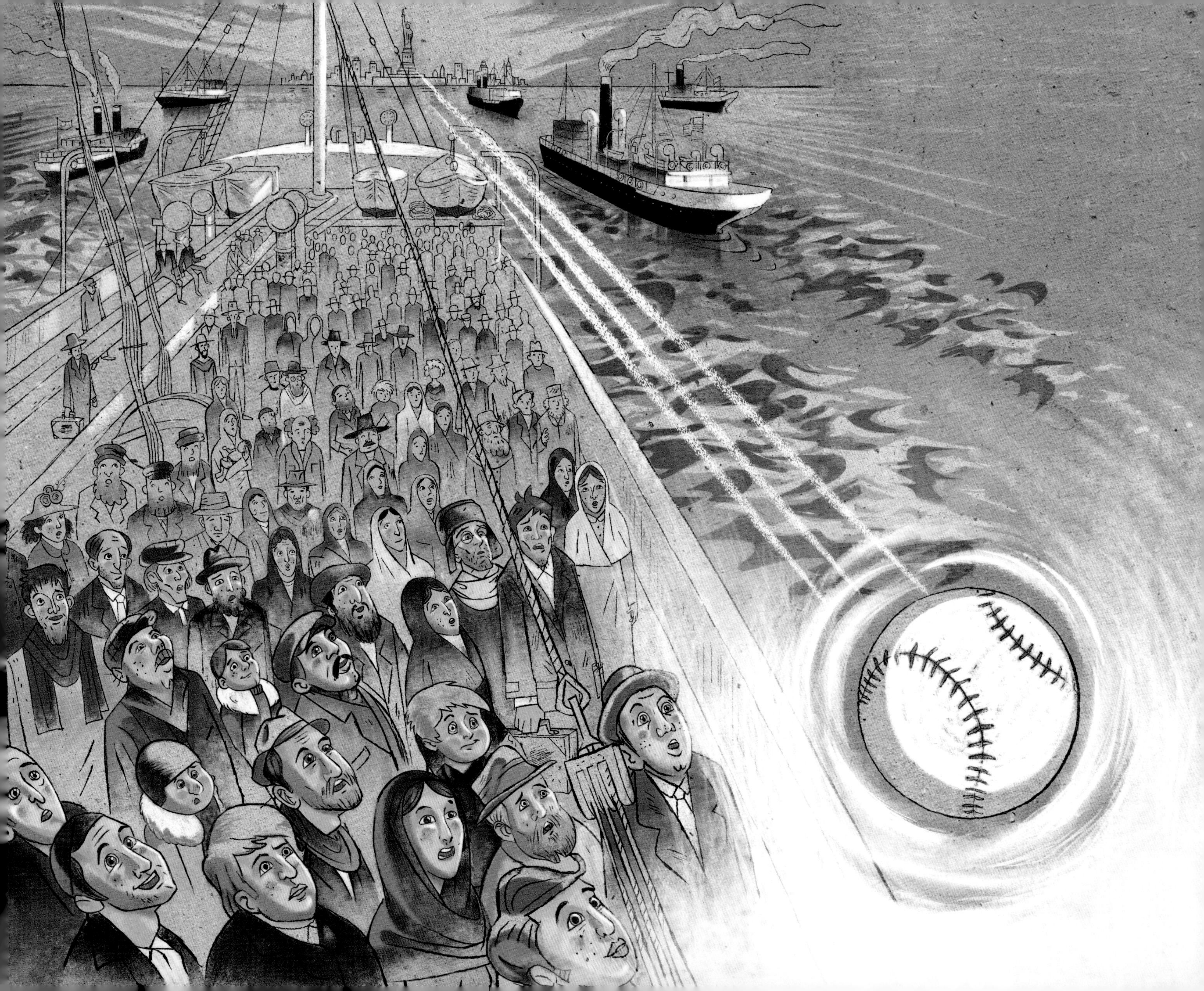